CYBORG LEGACY

CYBORG LEGACY

a Fallen Empire novel

LINDSAY BUROKER

FOREWORD

Thank you for picking up *Cyborg Legacy*. This is the ninth novel in my Fallen Empire universe, but it stars a new hero and is designed to stand alone. If you're a new reader, welcome! If you've read the original series, thanks for coming back for more. As I said, Jasim is a new hero, but fan-favorite Leonidas is along for the ride. He's still kicking butt, even if he has a few more gray hairs (don't mention those hairs, though—he's sensitive about them). For those keeping track, this adventure takes place about four years after the events of *End Game*. I hope you enjoy the story!

As always, I had help in putting this novel together. Please let me thank Sarah Engelke and Rue Silver, my tireless beta readers, Shelley Holloway, my equally tireless editor, and Tom Edwards, my cover designer (I'm not sure about his tiredness level, but he illustrates these covers very quickly, so it's possible he's a cyborg).

Now, please jump in…

CHAPTER ONE

A soft *hiss-thunk* sounded as Jasim Antar fastened his helmet, the final piece of his combat armor, and walked out of his cabin on the *Interrogator*. He headed for Navigation and Communications where his lone companion on the journey sat in the pilot's seat. Knitting. Jasim grabbed a blazer rifle from the weapons locker on the way into NavCom.

When he entered, Maddy lowered her long needles and an amorphous purple and green blob that would, he had been informed, grow into a scarf to match the hat she had already knitted him. Her gray hair was swept back with a clip, and she wore a loose sweater of her own design, the sleeves pushed up to her elbows, the front featuring a cheerful orange bird perched on a twig. The weapons belt secured at her waist, a blazer pistol longer than her forearm hanging in the holster, contrasted oddly with the otherwise kindly grandmother visage.

"Ready for a tough one, big man?" Maddy asked.

Jasim snorted. Big man. Hardly. When he'd applied to join the Cyborg Corps, back when the empire had dominated the system and the imperial army had been a great entity with headquarters on every planet, he'd cracked his spine trying to stand tall enough to make the minimum six-foot height requirement. He was an inch too short, and he was fairly certain the recruiting doctor had only allowed him in because the war had been ramping up, and he'd had a quota to make. Few men had been crazy enough to sign up for the extensive surgeries and body alterations that came with being turned into an imperial cyborg.

"I'm ready," Jasim said. He'd never thought he would miss the war and the killing—the sun gods knew he'd tried to get out of the unit more than once—but at least he'd had a purpose then. Now...

"I'll do my flyby to make sure the ship is there," Maddy said, turning toward the control panel. Her needles and project went into the yarn-filled knitting basket next to her seat.

"Don't get too close to the compound. He'll have enhanced hearing, just like me. I'd rather not warn him I'm coming by buzzing his living room window."

"You needn't tell me how to do my job, dear," Maddy said, swooping low over the tents, metal buildings, and salvage yards that dominated this part of Temperance. *Most* parts of Temperance. Targos Moon had not been doing well since the empire fell, with the dozens of governments that had sprouted up too busy squabbling over resources to worry about their people, and Temperance was controlled by a mafia clan that wasn't reputed to be any better. "I've been flying since before your mother was paddling your bare bottom."

"My mother died before I was old enough to need paddling. I grew up on the streets of New Jerome with my older sisters."

"Well, I'm sure paddling was involved. You have a naughty personality."

Jasim arched his eyebrows. "I'm certain I've never done anything to suggest that to you." Granted, he occasionally played a prank or two on those who deserved it, but even if Maddy had deserved pranks, he would be afraid to try anything on her, since she was his boss's mother-in-law. Any woman who cheerfully allowed her daughter to marry a man known as The Pulverizer was not to be trifled with.

"I've read your record. Your last pilot complained about run-ins with something called a whoopee cushion."

"Actually, it was a splat pad, and that was only one time. And he deserved it. He was smooching with a prostitute in NavCom when I was getting shot at and needed a pickup. I trust you won't be unreliable like that."

"I suppose that depends on how handsome the prostitutes here are." Maddy winked at him.

"Pilots," he grumbled. It didn't matter how many children or grandchildren they had. They were all half-crazy. If not all crazy. He wouldn't be surprised if Maddy came from the word *mad* rather than being a shortening of her name, Madeline.

He got another wink before Maddy returned her focus to the control panel. A three-legged dog roaming a street threw back his head and barked at them as they flew overhead. The cloudy green sky was clear of other spaceships. Few people had a reason to visit the unincorporated part of Temperance. Jasim wagered most of the citizens wished they lived somewhere else. Where else, he didn't know. Most former imperial citizens who hadn't turned traitor and fought for the Alliance now had trouble getting citizenship on their pretty core planets.

"There she is," Maddy said, nodding toward one of several holodisplays, this one showing the ship's port camera feed.

The sleek black hull of a ten-man star yacht rested on a dirt lot surrounded by a brick and barbed-wire fence. Less than a year old, the gleaming spaceship stuck out outrageously in the impoverished neighborhood. Jasim was surprised the locals hadn't broken it down into pieces to sell, but supposed the presence of the man living in the squat cinderblock structure attached to the yard might have intimidated them.

"What a beaut," Maddy said, eyeing the yacht. "I looked at the specs earlier. She's got real showers instead of saniboxes, and there are auto-massagers and saunas in the lavatories."

"You don't think The Pulverizer would put a sauna in the lav on this ship for you?" Jasim asked.

"Please, he's a scrimper. Besides, where would it go in that tiny lav? The toilet would have to be *inside* the sauna for it to fit. And an auto-massager?" She sighed wistfully and looked at Jasim's arms. "I'd ask you to put those meat slabs of yours to work in a useful manner, but I don't want to have my bones crushed."

"Meat slabs?"

"What do you call them?" She waved to his arms.

The armor hid the thick muscles at the moment, but Jasim supposed she'd seen him in a T-shirt often enough in the few weeks they had been working together to remember them well. He'd caught her investigating other parts of him, too, usually when she didn't think he was looking. It probably wasn't appropriate to think of his boss's mother-in-law as lecherous.

"I call them *arms*," Jasim said.

"How insufficient." Maddy whistled cheerfully and adjusted their course. "I'll get within a half-mile, and you'll have to rappel out. There's no place to land, and I wouldn't want to in this neighborhood even if I could. Probably wouldn't take the hoodlums thirty seconds before they descended on us and tried to tear off the panels for scrap."

"Just open the hatch, and I'll jump out." Jasim waved at the altimeter to indicate that he could handle the thirty- or forty-foot drop.

"Ah, right. I forgot. You're like an android."

Jasim frowned but didn't bother correcting her. He'd tried numerous times in the years since the war ended, but he hadn't had much luck changing people's assumptions about cyborgs. At least she didn't call him "mech," the derisive nickname many people had for cyborgs. Not that many used the term to their faces.

"Just fly over one of the streets," Jasim said, turning toward the exterior hatch that opened up from the ship's single corridor. "Preferably not one of those alleys full of dog piss and potholes."

"I've been to Temperance before. I don't think that's *dog* piss."

"Lovely."

Jasim walked the three steps to the hatch—the *Interrogator* was a modern ship with a fast engine, good shields, and impressive weapons, but it was definitely not luxurious or large. As he waited for Maddy to find a spot, he silently ordered his helmet display to turn on. The neural net touching his scalp in several spots read the command and obeyed, and readings that ranged from sensor data about his surroundings, to the suit's integrity, to his body's vital statistics appeared along the sides of his faceplate. They did not interfere with his vision, and it was easy to look through them instead of focusing on them during a battle. Everything appeared normal, and his heartbeat thumped along at a perfectly normal rhythm despite his nervousness about the target he would confront on this particular mission.

He checked his rifle and the smaller blazer weapons that could pop out of the arms of his suit on command. He doubted thugs would leap out at him as soon as he landed—most people fled from men wearing the distinctive red combat armor of the Cyborg Corps—but when he was operating on his own like this, he couldn't be too careful. Maddy might provide some aerial backup if he got in trouble, but that wasn't her job. She was supposed to fly him to the deadbeats, tow the ships they collected if necessary, arrange to have them transported back to headquarters, and fly him to the next mission. That was it. She also, Jasim suspected, reported back to her son-in-law regularly and would let The Pulverizer know if Jasim absconded with any of the goods he was supposed to be retrieving.

A boom came from outside, and the ship tilted alarmingly.

The stabilizers in Jasim's leg armor kept him upright without trouble, but the litany of un-grandmotherly curses that came from NavCom was alarming. He'd never heard her denigrate the size of the reproductive organs of all three sun gods before, not all at once.

"Problem?" Jasim asked.

"Some idiot with a grenade launcher is firing at us from a rooftop." Even as she finished speaking, the *Interrogator* banked hard.

This time, Jasim braced himself by pressing his gauntleted hands against the bulkhead. In space, artificial gravity would usually keep the ship stable, but down here, it was more akin to being in an airplane. An airplane that was under fire.

As the ship rose and looped back the way it had come, Maddy said, "Hold back on opening the hatch. I had to raise the shields."

As the deck shifted and tilted, Jasim made his way back to NavCom and looked at the view screen. He was in time to see a pack of men and women in baggy, mismatched clothing pointing weapons at them from the flat rooftop of a three-story tenement building. There was more than one grenade launcher among the group, along with everything from blazer rifles to shotguns to a longbow that someone looked to have made by hand. Its owner couldn't have been more than twelve.

Maddy wore a determined expression as she arrowed the ship toward the rooftop.

"You're not going to fire, are you?" Jasim gripped her shoulder, careful, as always, not to squeeze too hard. In addition to having the strength that his cyborg implants gave him, combat armor amplified the wearer's power.

"Nobody fires at The Pulverizer's ships without receiving retaliation," Maddy said, speaking it like a mantra. Maybe it was underlined in the company rulebook somewhere.

"You'll blow up that whole building."

"It might improve the neighborhood."

"There'll be people in it. Women and children, maybe. *Grandchildren*," he added, since she had mentioned having more than a dozen of those herself.

She kept flying, looking determined to blow up the entire building, if not the city block.

"Maddy," he said quietly, giving her a slight warning squeeze, even though threatening her would not be good for his career. He did not want to wrest the controls from her, but he would if he had to.

She growled, but did not fire as they swooped low over the rooftop. The *Interrogator* received more fire from the group of thugs, bullets and blazer beams pinging off their shields. Those weapons wouldn't do any damage. The grenades were another story. Maddy banked hard to avoid another one that was launched from the rooftop. It blew up to their starboard side amid a cloud of black smoke. The ship rocked, but the shields remained near full power.

"What kind of cyborg soldier *are* you?" Maddy asked, scowling at him as she swooped left and right to make a challenging target.

"A retired one," Jasim said, though it seemed an odd word to use. After all, he was only twenty-seven. He'd only been in for three years before the war ended. "And not one who ever targeted civilians," he added firmly.

"That's not what the stories about the Cyborg Corps say."

Jasim pressed his lips together. "I know what the stories say."

"I wasn't just spouting nonsense back there. We have a company policy that anyone who tries to damage one of our ships or one of our people gets *handled*—like a straw bale on a rifle range. Our logo is on the side of the ship where anyone can see it. We can't let word get back of our weakness. The Pulverizer has a reputation."

"I'm aware of it. Drop me on the roof, and I'll deal with them." Jasim felt like a thug when he said such things, but he couldn't object too much to using force on people who shot at him. He just didn't want to take out innocent people lounging on their couches and reading news holos on the first floor. Not everyone who lived in this neighborhood was a felon. He knew all too well what it was like to grow up in a place like this and have no way to escape it.

"I'll have to lower shields for you to jump out," Maddy said.

"I'll be quick." He released her shoulder with a pat and headed back to the hatch.

"I'll have Earl send the repair bill to you."

"Earl?"

"My son-in-law."

"No wonder he goes by The Pulverizer."

"No insulting the family, cyborg, or you might not get picked up again."

"I'll remember that." Jasim returned to the hatch and touched the control panel on the bulkhead beside it, calling up the forward camera on the display. Between the shock absorbers in his armor and his mostly synthetic bones and joints, he could survive if he jumped and missed the rooftop, but seeing him splat against a brick wall wouldn't drive fear into the hearts of their attackers. "Ready when you are."

"Lowering shields," Maddy said.

The people on the rooftop jumped and pointed, aiming their weapons eagerly. They probably couldn't believe the ship was coming back so they would get another chance at it. Missing sauna or not, Jasim knew the *Interrogator's* parts could bring in good money on the black market. Or maybe the *farmers'* market—he doubted the authorities cared much about policing illegal salvage here, and it wouldn't surprise him to see stolen fuel cells and tube couplers for sale in a kiosk next to tomatoes and asteroid fruit.

Jasim tapped the controls, and the hatch slid open. Maddy hadn't slowed down for her approach, and wind buffeted his armor and tugged at the rifle slung across his torso on a strap.

He was about to jump out when Maddy shouted, "One's firing," and banked hard.

Jasim, already crouched to spring, had to adjust his aim. He jumped from the ship, leaping outward instead of simply dropping down. More wind railed at him but not enough to alter the descent of a two-hundred-pound man in full combat armor.

As he landed on the corner of the rooftop, he planned to charge straight toward the men and women and deal with them as rapidly as possible—his armor could deflect a lot of bullets and blazer bolts, but it wasn't as impervious as the ship's shields and would weaken eventually. But part of the old building gave way under his feet, and he had to react quickly to keep from plummeting through to the top floor. His charge turned into a roll away from the hole crumbling open underneath him, and crimson blazer bolts streaked past above him.

"Combat armor," someone whispered, Jasim's superior hearing catching the words from across the rooftop. "It's worth a fortune."

"Get him. Get him good!"

Jasim recovered from his ungainly landing, leaped to his feet, and raced toward the pack. Not everyone agreed with the speakers, and some of the smarter thugs were already scattering, eyes wide as they took in his red armor. Several, however, stood their ground, unleashing their rifles and pistols at him. There wasn't any cover on the rooftop, except for an open trapdoor that didn't look like it could take a windy day, much less weapons fire. Jasim didn't bother dodging, but he kept an eye on the readout on his faceplate, reporting on hits and giving him armor integrity updates. He almost laughed when a crooked arrow bounced off his shoulder.

He crossed the roof in a second and leaped into the middle of his foes. Even without the combat armor, his enhancements gave him speed and strength that unaltered humans couldn't match. He knocked two men off the roof and grabbed the grenade launcher from a third before the thugs registered what was going on and tried to run out of his reach. He gripped the grenade launcher in both hands, and metal squealed as the frame bent, then snapped. He threw the pieces to the ground and knocked more people from the rooftop, some flying twenty feet before they tumbled over the side and to the ground below.

Screams of pain came up from below, and he had no doubt there would be broken bones, if not worse. But he knew Maddy was right. They couldn't let the company be a target, and a strong showing here might mean he would face less opposition as he walked toward the target's house. Word traveled fast, especially in run-down neighborhoods like this.

He let the people who ran get away, even though he could have easily caught up with them. Only the fools who were determined to keep fighting sealed their fate. He knocked them across the rooftop or tossed them off the building with the others. When he'd first received his cyborg implants, he'd been delighted at his newfound strength, his ability to thwart all those people who had once bullied him, but years of war and killing and walking across the battlefields of the maimed and fallen had bled the satisfaction out of him. Now, there were far more regrets than delights. Still, he did his job, because it was the only one he had.

Soon, only one opponent remained on his feet. The boy with the home-made bow and arrows. Dirt smeared his grimy face and hands, but it did not hide the terror in his eyes or the shake to his hands.

As Jasim strode toward him, he expected the kid to drop his bow and run. But he held his ground.

"You keep coming, and I'll shoot."

His bravery surprised Jasim, and he admired it, even if it was only likely to get the kid killed around here. Jasim wished he could take him away from the neighborhood or impart some message to him, some advice to help him survive to adulthood and find a better future. After all, that was what Jasim had gone to school for after the war. Teaching children. Helping them. But how could he reconcile that with his current job, one that demanded he not allow slights against his boss—or his boss's ship? If nothing else, he should offer a few tips on how to survive in an unfriendly world. That way, the boy might be wise enough to run the next time.

When he didn't stop advancing, the kid was true to his threat and fired.

Jasim caught the arrow out in front of him, before the tip would have bounced off his chest piece. He gentled his grip so that he didn't snap the wood. Finally, the boy seemed to get an inkling of what sort of foe he faced. He lowered his bow. Still, he didn't run. He stared defiantly.

Jasim stopped in front of him. "I have a couple of suggestions for you."

The boy blinked. Apparently, that wasn't what he'd expected to hear.

"First off," Jasim said, "I recommend that when someone in combat armor enters your neighborhood, you run. Far and fast. You can't spend the money you think you could get from selling his armor if you're dead, eh?"

The boy's expression grew mulish.

"But if you *can't* run, because you're a part of one of the gangs and they're putting pressure on you…" Jasim lifted his eyebrows, wondering if that was the case, or if the kid just wasn't that smart. "You better have some rust bangs."

The boy's expression changed, his face wrinkling in confusion.

"They're sort of like grenades," Jasim said, "but when they explode, they spit out a kind of acid that can eat through spaceship hulls, combat armor, and just about anything with a metal component. It doesn't feel too good on skin either."

"Where..."

"You'd have to find a military surplus store to get some around here, I imagine, but I've heard of people making homemade versions out of local ingredients."

"What *kinds* of ingredients?"

"Well, you'd have to study some chemistry to learn that. Can you read? Do you go to school?"

The boy hesitated. "I *did*. But my mom needs... *stuff*, and you can't make money around here from what dumb things they tell you in school."

"You sure? I figure it'd be useful around here to know how to make rust bangs. Smoke bombs too. Those aren't that hard to make. A little chemistry..."

Now, a speculative expression grew on the boy's face.

Jasim wondered if he was planting the seed that school could be useful or if he was just making the kid think about muggings and robberies his gang could commit with rust bangs and smoke bombs.

"Teachers usually have certain things they have to teach you," Jasim said, "but if you show an interest in something else and ask for help with learning about it, they'll be happy to give that help."

Jasim's comm beeped, reminding him that Maddy was waiting for him. He held out the arrow to the boy to return it. He accepted it distractedly, as if lost in thought. Maybe he was imagining himself hurling smoke bombs.

Jasim almost told the kid his own story, of how he'd survived a neighborhood just like this, if not one that was worse than this, until he had been old enough to enlist in the imperial army. But where was the happy ending? It had gotten him off the streets, and he'd finished his degree after the war, but only to learn that nobody would hire a cyborg to do anything that didn't involve brutalizing people. Almost ten years after he'd escaped his childhood, he was a thug, working in the same kinds of places that he'd grown up in.

"Thanks," the boy said, scampering away, his arrow in hand.

Jasim left, having no way to know if anything he had said would make a difference to the kid. He walked to the edge of the rooftop and leaped down to the street. The pained groans of those he'd thrown off the building drifted to his ears, making him wince.

Another comm beep sounded.

"Antar?" Maddy asked.

"Yes?"

"You're less than a half a mile from the target's house. I'm transmitting a map."

"Understood."

The map popped up on the side of his faceplate, showing his location and the target's address.

"Be careful dealing with him," Maddy said. "It'll be a lot more challenging than those scrawny thugs."

"I know," Jasim said, turning up an alley in the direction the map indicated. "I remember him from the Corps."

"Ah. I'd wondered if you might."

Jasim said nothing else. He didn't look forward to coming face-to-face with someone else in red combat armor. Sergeant Matt Adams, a man who'd referred to Jasim as "Shorty." A man who would have the strength to kill him. Jasim hoped it wouldn't come to that, that Adams would agree that he was a year behind on the payments for his yacht and accept that it had to go back to the dealership, but Jasim remembered Adams's temper, remembered that he liked to fight and that he liked to kill. He doubted very much that this would be easy.

CHAPTER TWO

Jasim could feel eyes upon him as he turned onto the final street, old pavement crumbling underneath his boots. Ratty curtains shifted in glassless windows, and shadows moved behind partially boarded-up doors. Though aware of the watchers, he faced forward, not overly worried about them. His target was another matter.

Sergeant Adams's home loomed at the end of a pothole-filled cul-de-sac, looking more like a warehouse than a dwelling. Jasim supposed a house wouldn't have come with a large enough yard to park one's luxury yacht in.

His instincts told him to leap up to one of the high second-story windows, work a shutter lose, and slip in that way, completely avoiding the target if possible. Indeed, he spotted a window where the shutter already stood open. Invitingly. But The Pulverizer, despite his ominous reputation, employed a system of collecting delinquent loans and valuables that obeyed the local laws on planets and moons that had them. Jasim first had to knock on the target's door, inform him that his loan was past due, and ask for the return of the spaceship. If the target did not prove amenable, then he could use force. Murders were unacceptable unless they happened as a result of self-dense. Apparently, The Pulverizer had lawyers who could make charges disappear if the claim of self-defense was debatable and someone was left to press charges. Jasim had not tested that. He had no wish to test it here, either, and he eyed that open window with longing.

Bracing himself, he knocked on the wooden double-doors, the metal rivets lining the frame as large as his fist. The walls on most of the buildings on the street were covered with graffiti. Adams's place was old and dirty, but there were no signs of vandalism. Everyone in the neighborhood likely knew who and what lived here.

After waiting for a minute, Jasim knocked again. It crossed his mind to slip around back, leap the fence, and use his lock-thwarting repo kit to simply take the ship, but he'd already walked through the alley behind the compound and heard the faint hum of a forcefield. The brick and barbed wire were clearly for show, with more deadly security measures waiting unseen. It would be safer to walk through the house, out the back door, and into the yard.

But nobody answered the door to let him in—or oppose his wish to come in.

Jasim tried the latch, certain it would be locked. He had a kit that could neutralize technological as well as physical locks, and was halfway to reaching for it, but before he could pull it out, the latch gave way and the door creaked open.

"Huh."

He waited for the telltale thud of footsteps from someone running toward him. All he heard was the buzz of flies. He sniffed before remembering that his helmet would filter out smells—along with any toxic substances that might be in the air. Still, as he walked into a cavernous warehouse-like room half-filled with stacks of crates, he began to suspect that he might not have to face Adams after all.

A metal door stood closed along the back wall—it should lead out to the yard—but Jasim turned toward a hallway off to the side, assuming it led to offices or maybe a living area.

The buzz of flies grew louder. Dim light filtered through the shuttered windows, but there were not any lamps on. There were not any lamps at *all*, or any sign that electricity was present in this part of the city. Adams must have a generator out back to power the forcefield.

Old wooden floorboards creaked under Jasim's armored boots. Doors lined the hallway on both sides, some closed and others open. He passed a lavatory and an office, where a desk was piled high with what looked like bills, paper ones. He didn't see a netdisc or any hint that the warehouse was hooked up to the sys-net. He opened two more doors, one to a kitchen area and one to an empty bedroom. The last door at the end of the hallway was open.

By now, he didn't expect to encounter anyone. He was already feeling pleased, for The Pulverizer's rules allowed him to take the yacht if it was present and the owner wasn't, merely leaving a note that it had been repossessed by request of the title holder. When he walked into the back room, it was dark, and surprise jolted him when he almost stumbled over something on the floor. Flies flew up, one bouncing off his faceplate. Jasim barely noticed, his eyes focused now on the unmoving man sprawled before him.

Clad in nothing but his underwear, the man lay between the bunk and the door, bed sheets tangled in a heap near his feet. His gray eyes were frozen open in death, a pained grimace stamped on his face. Deep, bloody gashes had been cut all over his arms, legs, and chest. For a second, Jasim wondered if he had stumbled across some strange ritualistic murder—or sacrifice—to one of the obscure elder gods. But he didn't have to look at the placement of those scars for long to realize what had happened. Someone had cut out the man's—the cyborg's—implants.

Though his stomach twisted, Jasim leaned down to push apart one of the gashes so he could be certain. Yes, a grayish implant responsible for strengthening a cyborg's extensor digitorum muscle should have been in that spot, and it was gone.

Jasim leaned back, frowning. One of the man's burly, heavily muscled arms stretched toward a corner of the room where a large, red metal box rested on the floor. An armor case, identical to the one that held Jasim's armor when he wasn't using it.

"Someone took your implants but not your armor?" Jasim muttered. Yes, the implants would be worth more, but the armor would be a lot easier to take and sell. Someone had to know exactly what he was doing to extract the implants without damaging them. Not to mention that someone had to be able to kill a cyborg, no easy feat, to gain access to them.

Jasim walked to the case and lifted the lid. The entire set of armor rested inside in pieces, neatly put away into the proper slots. Odd.

"Well, it doesn't look like you're going to object to me taking your ship back," Jasim said quietly, looking down at the man's face. Shaggy hair fell across the forehead, and a thick beard hid the mouth and jaw, but Jasim recognized him regardless. He hadn't liked the man, but his squad had fought alongside Adams's squad more than once. No question. This was Sergeant Matt Adams. His target.

All Jasim's job required of him was to reclaim the yacht, and he could have headed into the yard and done that without looking around further, but he couldn't help wondering what had killed the man. It was more than idle curiosity. Seeing one of his fellow cyborgs dead made him uneasy. He found himself looking around for threats, for something that might endanger him too. Even when they were clad in nothing but underwear, cyborgs weren't easy to kill, and it was a foregone conclusion that Adams had been dead before the implants had been removed.

Jasim knelt to look at the body more closely. The pectoral gashes were long, but hadn't gone through to bone and organs. Blood smeared Adams's body and stained the floor, but there weren't any bullet or blazer wounds, or any deep punctures.

Adams might have had a heart attack, but the man was only about thirty, so that seemed unlikely. Even though all the tinkering the imperial doctors had done to create their cyborgs had resulted in some metabolic oddities and a shortened lifespan—something the recruiting fliers hadn't mentioned—they rarely dropped dead from heart attacks, at least not in their thirties. Few lived to old age, but as far as Jasim knew, that was because they were picked for dangerous jobs and met violent ends long before they were old enough to retire from service. The man who'd been the Cyborg Corps commander when Jasim had served, Colonel Adler, had been one of the oldest in the unit at nearly forty. Jasim wondered what had happened to him after the war. He would be closer to forty-five now. Was he still alive somewhere? What work had he found after the fall of the empire? Something more glamorous than repossessing people's belongings?

Jasim rolled the body over, looking for deadly wounds on the other side. Adams wasn't stiff, and it looked like rigor mortis had come and gone, so this must have happened a few days ago. He was surprised nobody in the neighborhood had been in to loot Adams's belongings, especially with that window open and the front door unlocked.

Jasim didn't see sign of broken bones or any suggestion that there had been a fight. He magnified his faceplate to examine Adams's neck, ignoring the cuts on the sides. Was it possible someone had strangled him? It was hard to imagine someone even getting his hands around the thickly muscled neck. Even someone in combat armor would be hard-pressed to fight off the defenses of a cyborg long enough to actually finish strangling him. Could he have been attacked by a fellow cyborg? Maybe he'd rubbed more than the titleholder of that yacht the wrong way with his inability to stay current on his payments.

"What's this?" Jasim murmured, leaning closer and touching the front of Adams's neck.

There was a tiny puncture in the skin near a tendon. It almost could have passed for a pore, but the hole went deeper than that. If Jasim hadn't magnified his faceplate and looked specifically at Adams's neck, he never would have noticed it.

He leaned back on his heels. "Did someone poison you in bed, Sergeant?"

Once again, Jasim peered about the room, as if what or who had done the deed might be lurking nearby, but only flies buzzed around. Whoever had done this had come and gone. A stealthy assassin, or maybe even a drone that had been sent in with cutting tools. That might explain why the implants had been taken but not the armor. A drone would simply have orders to perform one duty, not loot a place for all its valuables. Usually, a cyborg would hear the soft buzz of something flying and wake up, but an empty bottle of vodka rested on the table by the bed. Adams might have been sleeping more deeply than usual.

Jasim sighed. If he were on a more civilized world, he could call the police, someone who could perform an autopsy, and he could find out what poison had killed Adams. But there weren't police here. Just mafia thugs who enforced what passed for the law. And who *anywhere* would care that a former imperial cyborg had been killed? The Corps had been feared far and wide from its earliest inception, both by enemies and by loyal imperial subjects. They'd ruthlessly patrolled the empire, enforcing peace with violence, as they had been designed to do.

Jasim stood up. The word would get out soon enough, and the locals would swarm the place, taking Adams's armor and anything else of value.

"An ignoble end, my friend," he murmured.

He snorted softly. Friend? Surely Adams hadn't been that. Jasim had avoided the man whenever possible. But somehow, death erased distaste, reminding him more of how they had been alike than how they had been different.

Jasim tapped the armor case in the corner, activating the hover ability. He didn't like the idea of the locals fighting over it to sell it, so he would take it, along with the ship. The yacht had to go back to the dealership, but he would look up Adams, see if he had any living family, and return it to them if he did. Times were hard for most people now. Let his relatives sell the armor if they wanted.

Technically, the armor belonged to the empire, but after the final battle, there had been no supply sergeant left in headquarters to turn it in to—there had been no *headquarters* at all. As far as Jasim knew, all the cyborgs who had survived had kept their armor.

As he headed back through the warehouse, the armor case hissing softly as it floated behind him, Jasim commed the *Interrogator*. Chances were, what had killed Adams would remain a mystery, even if he tried to investigate it, but he knew someone who could find Adams's family more easily than he could—assuming she didn't charge a fortune.

"Everything all right?" Maddy asked.

"Yes…and no. Will you get in touch with Arlen McCall for me?"

"The weird skip tracer whose dog is more likely to answer the comm than she is?"

"That's her. Just send a message, ask her if she can look up our target and find out if Adams has any family and if so, where they are."

"You killed him?" Maddy asked, no hint of reproof in her voice.

"No. Someone else did. Three days ago would be my guess."

"And they didn't take his yacht?"

"I don't think they took anything," Jasim said, glancing at the crates in the warehouse.

"Give me a couple minutes."

Jasim tapped the button to unlock the back door, and it opened without any security requirements. Apparently, if one got past the cyborg, exploring the rest of the compound was easy. He found the button to lower the forcefield protecting the ship and walked to the sleek yacht resting in the dust. There wasn't so much as a dent. Aside from missing payments, Adams looked to have taken care of his baby. Maybe he had enjoyed the auto-massager.

As he approached, Jasim hoped it would be as easy to get into—it wasn't uncommon for people to booby trap their ships when they knew the repo men were coming. If they couldn't have it, they didn't want anyone else to have it either.

But he boarded it without trouble. The hatch opened welcomingly for him, and the AI called him "sir" when he walked up the ramp. Already familiar with the layout and operations, he headed for the yacht's version of NavCom. He sat down and fired up the craft. His piloting skills were limited, and he wouldn't want to deal with the gravitational anomalies out in space between the system's three suns, but The Pulverizer had sent him to a quick training course, and he could get most vessels through local air and to the transport stations where they would be loaded with other freight and returned to their originators.

"Antar?" Maddy asked over his helmet comm. "You have your netdisc with you?"

"No, but my armor can hook up to the sys-net if there are local satellites that don't charge by the second."

"No promises about that, but your buddy is just over at Bronos Moon, so there wasn't much lag. Looks like she got your message immediately. Or the dog did. I'm not sure. But a text message came back through. I'll forward it to you right away."

"Right away?" Jasim asked. "Is there something alarming in it?"

"Only if you're a cyborg."

"Well, thank the sun gods there aren't any of those around here."

Maddy snorted. "You're an odd boy, big man, but I'm still going to finish knitting your scarf."

"The gods are shining triply upon me today," Jasim said, while holding back a grimace. The hat she had made him, a gift she had given him after their first mission together, made his head itch. And other body parts too.

Wool. Horrible stuff. He hoped whichever colonist had thought it would be a good idea to freeze sheep embryos and bring them on the voyage from Old Earth had fallen into a volcano and died as soon as he stepped out of his ship.

"Clearly," Maddy said. "Meet you at the transport station?"

"Yes." Jasim tapped the thruster controls and lifted the yacht into the air, hoping no more locals with grenade launchers would take pot shots at him.

His helmet beeped softly, and a message started to display on his faceplate. It paused after only a line. A polite flashing warning told him that he needed to pay to see the rest of it, and would he like to authorize charges?

"Authorize," he grumbled, wondering if the effort—and expense—to find Adams's family was worth it.

Yes, he decided. It was bad enough he was leaving the body behind, so they wouldn't be able to hold a proper funeral. But CargoExpress forbade the shipping of corpses, as he'd learned on another occasion, and he doubted The Pulverizer would authorize Maddy to take him on a two-week trip to deliver a body. Knowing the boss, he would have another assignment ready for Jasim before he had this yacht secured and ready to ship.

After informing him that funds were being withdrawn from his account, the message displayed.

> *Sergeant Matt Aaron Adams*, it read, *originally from Zeta Colony on Sherran Moon. Surviving family, grandmother Jessica Adams, Zeta Colony. Possibly more pertinent information? Fourth former Cyborg Corps soldier killed in the last month.*

Jasim blinked. "What?"

Of course, he did not receive an answer from the recorded message. But if McCall was on or orbiting Bronos Moon, he could get one soon if he sent the question to her. The message continued for a few more lines.

Others deceased: Mahir Abadi, Stefan Albrecht, José Luis Alvarado. I've attached a file with the reports. Most are just one-line obituaries. All of the cyborgs died of mysterious causes and in their sleep, and their implants were removed, presumably after the fact. Only Alvarado's death was investigated. He worked for Senator Bondarenko on Perun. An unidentified substance was found in his bloodstream, believed to be a poison or venom. You better watch out. You're an A too.

~McCall

"I'm an A too?" Jasim asked, puzzling over that before it dawned on him. His surname. Antar. All of the dead cyborgs' surnames started with the letter A. "What in the suns' fiery hells?"

Was someone going down the Cyborg Corps duty roster? And if so, *why*? If they were being targeted so their implants could be sold on the black market, what did the order of deaths matter? Wouldn't it be easier for the murderer to simply pick the closest cyborgs available?

A hollow chill went through him, and he was glad no thugs on rooftops fired at the yacht, because he was barely paying attention to his route. He had pulled a lot of guard shifts with Alvarado. They were next to each other on the roster. Did that mean *he* was the next target?

Jasim rubbed his face, not sure if he should flee to the far border worlds, go about his normal job while taking precautions, or try to find out who was behind this. The latter appealed to his sense of nobility, but where would he even start? McCall could perhaps help him with research, but who knew how much she would charge? He was surprised she hadn't mentioned a fee already. The Pulverizer always paid her invoices when they needed her to find people who had gone off the grid with their stolen belongings.

A bump behind his seat made Jasim jump. For a second, he thought someone had stowed away, but it was just Adams's armor case, still hovering where he'd left it after boarding. Seeing the cyborg armor jarred a new thought into his mind. An unsettling one.

Earlier, he had been wondering where his old battalion commander, Colonel Adler, had gone after the war. He was an A. Had he already been targeted? Already been killed? It could have happened somewhere remote and not been reported to the news organizations yet.

Jasim hadn't known the man well—in fact, he was somewhat terrified of him, both because of his reputation and because he'd made a bad impression on the colonel early during his enlistment—but maybe he would know what to do about all this. At the least, he should be warned that someone might be after him. If they hadn't already gotten him.

Trying to set aside that grim thought, Jasim recorded a message to send to McCall.

"Thanks for the help, McCall. Let me know how much I owe you for the information. And I have one more request. Can you find out where Colonel Hieronymus Adler is currently located?"

CHAPTER THREE

Hieronymus "Leonidas" Adler strode into NavCom on the old freighter he co-owned with the pilot—who was also his wife—Alisa. He touched her on the back of the head, letting his fingers linger while he glowered at the view screen. A converted transport ship had come into range of the rear camera. The vessel had been heavily modified, given extra shielding and enough weapons to blow a hole through a small moon. Perhaps a large moon.

"Our cargo is being threatened, my stalwart business companion," Alisa said, not appearing overly worried as she smiled up at him.

After they'd married, she had given him half of the shipping business she'd formed, even though his entrepreneurial aspirations were primarily focused on keeping pirates, mafia, thieves, and other thugs off the ship and away from their cargo. And his family. He still thought of himself as the security officer, one who occasionally put his engineering degree to work by installing upgrades to the clunky old ship.

"Have they commed us?" he asked.

"They're just admiring our sexy ass right now." Alisa raised her eyebrows, perhaps inviting a comment about the irresistible appeal of her backside.

Normally, he would make it—and agree with the sentiment—but when trouble loomed, he preferred to stay focused on that. He was never one to underestimate enemies, especially when their ship, the *Star Nomad*, had considerably fewer weapons and probably couldn't outrun that vessel. He had more than cargo to protect. Jelena, Alisa's daughter who had also become a daughter to him, and their twin girls were on the ship, along with the rest of their crew and comrades.

"They're matching our speed right now?" Leonidas asked.

"They are." Alisa turned back to the control panel, not appearing offended by his preference to stay focused. After more than four years together, she knew him well. "I see you've come prepared for action." She waved toward his armored chest. He wore his full suit, save for the helmet tucked under his arm, and he had a rifle slung over his shoulder.

"I'm always prepared for action."

"I've noticed that about you." Her smile turned a touch lascivious as she winked at him. "It's one of the reasons I said yes so quickly when you asked me to marry you."

She understood his preference for focus, but that didn't keep her from deploying *her* preference for irreverent comments, no matter how dire the situation. He wouldn't have it any other way. He enjoyed their life together, even if endlessly traveling on a freighter, hauling cargo from moon to planet to station, sometimes made him miss the excitement of his days in the Cyborg Corps. In addition to the constant action, he'd mattered to a lot of people then. Now, nobody outside of this ship relied upon him. Sometimes, he wondered if he'd made a mistake in retiring. Not that there had been much choice after the empire fell. A couple of times, he'd been offered a position in the Alliance Army, but he had never considered the option. That would be betraying his principles, along with too many old friends, too many dead comrades.

He shifted his attention to the view screen again. Had the other ship drawn closer?

Anticipation for a possible battle thrummed through him. It had been *months* since anyone had picked a fight with the *Nomad*. He shouldn't long for battle, not when his family was aboard, but he couldn't help it. Even if wrangling children—in particular, two three-year-olds with a penchant for naughtiness—kept him on his toes, it wasn't the same. There was no outlet for his excess energy. Peering into forgotten nooks and opening cabinet doors to hunt for Maya and Nika's latest hiding spot wasn't the same as bashing enemy heads together in battle.

"They must know we've got a juicy payload," Alisa added, also watching the ship. "Isn't it funny how pirates always seem to know when our hold is empty versus when it's full?"

"I didn't realize tractors and backhoes constituted a *juicy* payload," Leonidas said, silently daring that ship to come forward and try to board them. That was his opportunity for battle. Oh, he didn't mind manning the co-pilot's seat and firing at enemies while Alisa dodged return fire, but he preferred to meet man or machine on an open deck, pitting himself against them and whatever secret weapons or sly tactics they brought with them.

"They're expensive tractors for a farmer on Epsilon Seven. I almost agreed to take on some cattle for a rancher there, too, but I was afraid the kids would get stepped on."

"Is that true? Or were you afraid Jelena would use her telepathy to befriend them and not want to let them go?"

Alisa smiled, but there was a hint of a grimace there too. "It's true that we don't need any more animals aboard."

Jelena had developed Starseer talents at a young age, and Alisa's father, Stanislav, was handling that part of her education. He hadn't yet convinced her that people were more interesting to befriend than animals. Maybe if Leonidas could telepathically communicate with dogs and chickens, he would find them more interesting too.

"Be glad she hasn't talked you into a horse yet," he said.

The comm flashed with an incoming message.

"Hah, that's them." Alisa slapped a button. "Greetings, stalkers. Have you commed to apologize for breathing up our butts for the last twenty minutes? Unless you're going to polish the rust off the hull while you're back there, we don't appreciate your presence."

"As charming to enemies as always," Leonidas murmured.

"Technically, they haven't committed to being enemies yet. That's just an armed ship without an ident flying too close for comfort."

"So your greeting was perfectly apt?"

"Perfectly." Alisa grinned at him. "Why don't you come closer? Right here next to me, please." She waved at the space between the seats, which happened to be within range of the comm camera if she turned on the video. Her eyes twinkled the way they did when she had some mischief in mind.

"Because," he said, bestirring himself to make a joke since she seemed in the mood for them, "you've been pining without my masculine presence close enough to touch?"

Jokes did not come naturally to him, whether it was a serious moment or not, and early in their relationship, he'd often frowned at her knack for sharing them at inappropriate times. But when he put forth the effort to make them, it always seemed to tickle her.

Indeed, her grin widened. "Always." She patted his armored wrist, then gripped it and pulled him up to the console. "Also, I want to transmit your image to our stalkers. The war may be long over, but seeing a cyborg in imperial combat armor still has a tendency to make people wet themselves."

"You know this from personal experience?" Leonidas allowed himself to be positioned in front of the camera, even though he would have preferred to be a surprise to their enemies if those pirates tried to board them. He knew Alisa hoped to forestall boarding or contact of any kind, and agreed that was a wise move, but against all logic, he craved that battle. Since their Starseer crew member Abelardus had married Young-hee and moved back to the Arkadius temple, he didn't have anyone on board he could challenge to sparring matches, not ones where he could potentially lose.

"I've passed a few puddles people left behind after you walked by," Alisa said.

"That's disgusting."

"You didn't think I saved my charms for my *enemies*, did you?" She reached for the comm, but paused halfway to the button. "Wait, can you turn sideways a bit, so that sticker isn't visible?"

He grunted and did so. Thanks to the children, his fearsome red combat armor was currently adorned with a prancing purple unicorn and a box of donuts that, when tapped, emitted the smell of baking pastries. Jelena had started the trend years earlier, and just when he'd thought she had grown past the age of stickers, she'd taught the twins the delight of pasting them on his armor. And most of the rest of the freighter too.

"And maybe put your helmet on?" Alisa added, waving at his head.

He narrowed his eyes to slits. "You better not be pointing at my gray hairs."

"I think there are more of them today than there were yesterday."

"Because I had to get up to round up the twins in the middle of the night. Twice. They decided to go camping in engineering by flashlight.

Apparently, Ostberg leaves cookies down there sometimes, and they know it."

"You're blaming the children for your hair? You commanded hundreds of men before you met me. Surely, that must have been more trying than being a father to small children."

"Well, they are *your* children."

"And yours. I refuse to believe my genes are more troublesome than yours."

"I don't know how you can say that with a straight face," Leonidas said, resting a hand on the back of her head again, tempted to remove his gauntlet so he could feel her silky hair against his skin. But he had better look fierce to scare off the pirates first. He lowered his hand and gave the camera a hard look. He did *not* put his helmet on. His gray hairs were just as fierce as he was.

Alisa didn't manage to keep her face straight. That grin crept out again. Shaking her head, she tapped the comm. But the other ship banked, thrusters flaring orange as it streaked off in another direction.

"What happened?" she asked. "I hadn't shown you off yet."

Leonidas, his sensitive ears catching footfalls and a familiar jangle of metal in the corridor behind them, could guess.

"Did I hear my family's genes being insulted?" Stanislav asked, stepping into NavCom.

"Leonidas thinks our children's troublemaking tendencies come from our side of the family," Alisa said, looking back, then looking Stanislav up and down. "I can't imagine why."

About a year ago, Stanislav had, at Alisa's urging, purchased some "normal" clothing, and had stopped wearing his black Starseer robe all the time. Unfortunately, he had done his shopping on the ranching planet of Epsilon Seven, choosing some of the preferred wear of the hands there, including snagor-hide boots and chaps over denim trousers. Today, he was also wearing one of the plaid shirts and a wide-brimmed hat that served no discernible purpose on a spaceship. Alisa dropped her face into her hand often when he walked by in the full getup.

"I must argue that my genes are not troublesome," Stanislav said. "I just informed those pirates that we have three Starseers on board, as well as a cyborg in full imperial combat armor. They seemed alarmed by hearing my voice in their heads and decided to practice their ruthless ways elsewhere."

"*Three* Starseers?" Alisa asked. "You, Ostberg, and are you counting Jelena? She's only twelve."

"Almost thirteen, as she'll be quick to inform you. And she can convince the geese to attack strangers en masse. She practically qualifies as a military officer."

"Those geese don't need convincing to attack. I was walking toward engineering with a sandwich the other day, and they came after me. En masse. I had to throw half my sandwich at them to get them to leave me alone."

"They do like bread," Stanislav said, inclining his head and walking out again. Spurs on his boots jangled as he left.

Leonidas gazed wistfully toward the departing ship.

"Sad that you didn't get a battle?" Alisa asked. Yes, she knew him well.

But he wasn't sure if he should admit that he had longed for potentially deadly action.

"Just lamenting that I donned my armor for no reason," he murmured.

"You could cruise through the children's cabin, so they can put some fresh stickers on you."

He gave her the flat look that comment deserved, then pushed his hand through his short hair. His short *graying* hair. He grimaced. How much longer would he be fit for battle? What if he had, even now, lost his edge? He trained with his hover pads, but that wasn't the same as fighting living, thinking enemies.

Noticing Alisa gazing thoughtfully at him, perhaps a bit worriedly at him, Leonidas tried to wipe his face of whatever emotions were drifting across it.

"Better that we didn't have anyone trying to kill us today," he said with a firm nod. "If nothing else, it's good to know that my armor still fits." He patted his stomach. "I don't follow the strict exercise routine I once did, after all."

"Yes, you're down to three hours a day in the gym. It's shameful."

"When we weren't engaged in combat missions, we worked out five to six hours a day in the Corps, in addition to constant drilling. And we ate fewer brownies." Admittedly, the lack of good food was not something he missed about the military. He was secretly glad "Uncle Tommy," as the kids called him, hadn't left the ship after he started making good money selling his sauces all across Aldrin's moons. He kept saying that once he made inroads into Alliance restaurants and stores, he would buy a place of his own somewhere, but for now, he was still doing his tinkering in the *Nomad's* upgraded kitchen. It didn't hurt that his assistant and girlfriend, Tanya, had been born on a space station and actually preferred being on a ship to sucking dirt planetside, as she said.

"I can't believe you weren't miserable," Alisa said. "I'd—"

The comm flashed again, and Leonidas felt a hopeful twinge. Maybe the pirates, once they'd escaped the range of Stanislav's mental manipulation, had realized that they did indeed want to make trouble.

"It's a recorded message from…Targos Moon," Alisa said.

Leonidas's hope died out.

"And it's for you," she added.

"Oh?" he asked, a touch warily.

Usually when people contacted him, they were imperial loyalists who wanted to bring him into some scheme to oust the Alliance from power and retake what rightfully belonged to the empire. Occasionally, they asked him to help, but usually, they just wanted to know where Prince Thorian was. Something he did not, at present, know. Not that he would have told them, regardless. Even though the border moons and planets were still lawless, or ruled by mafia families or corporate powerhouses, the Alliance had extended its government from the three core planets it had claimed at the end of the war to six and was gradually pushing its influence farther out into the system. It would be difficult now for the empire to gather enough forces to defeat them, and it would involve another long war. For all that he craved the challenges of battle, he didn't want to see millions more killed in another system-wide conflict.

"The name is Jasim Antar," Alisa said. "Do you want to take it in private?"

"Corporal Antar?" Leonidas frowned, the name pinging in his memory, but not with any warmth. "What does *he* want? That kid was a prankster on his best day and whined to Mental Health Services to try to get released from his contract and discharged on his worst."

"A prankster? I like him already."

"He set a whoopee cushion on someone's seat at an imperial function. He claimed it was for a sergeant who was pestering him. One of the emperor's aides sat on it."

Alisa's eyes crinkled at the corners. "Can I invite him for dinner?"

"If he's on Targos Moon, that's a long flight for someone to come to dinner." And even though Leonidas missed his unit at times, he had no wish to share a meal with one of the rejects from it. Why didn't the other officers or senior sergeants he'd fought with for years ever comm him?

Because most of them were dead, he admitted morosely.

"Beck's food is worth the trip," Alisa said.

Sighing, Leonidas sat in the co-pilot's seat and waved for her to play the message. He hoped he wouldn't regret it. "Whatever he has to say, you're welcome to hear it."

Alisa had fought in the Alliance and remained loyal to them—something she and Leonidas had never seen eye-to-eye on—and he knew it made her uneasy when his old imperial acquaintances got in touch with him. She must worry that some day the offer would be right, and he would run off with them to start a revolution. If he'd intended to run off with anyone, it would have been with Thorian, back before he'd married Alisa. He had been tempted when the ten-year-old prince asked him to come along and be his military advisor, and sometimes, he wondered what might have come of that if he'd agreed, but the idea of not having Alisa and the children in his life was too unappealing to contemplate for long.

A stiff-looking, bronze-skinned man with shoulder-length black hair appeared on the comm monitor. Even though it was a recording, Leonidas almost snapped at him to cut that mess so it would be in compliance with regulations. He snorted at himself. Old habits died hard.

"Colonel Adler, sir," the message started, and Leonidas slumped back in the seat, certain this would indeed turn into some request for him to join in with a secret plot. He was, however, surprised that Antar would be involved in any such thing. He had been an adequate enough soldier when the fighting started, but it had always been clear that he felt he'd made a mistake and didn't want to be there. Why would some loyalists choose him to be part of their plot? Simply because he was a cyborg?

"I hope this message finds you well," Antar went on. "And alive."

Alisa's eyebrows rose.

"I don't know if you keep track of the old unit at all," Antar said, "or have heard about the murders of Abadi, Albrecht, Alvarado, and Adams."

Alisa turned her raised eyebrows toward Leonidas. Frowning, he shook his head. He hadn't heard anything about murders, but before picking up the tractors, the *Nomad* had been way out by the Trajean Asteroid Belt, delivering machinery to a mining company. It took days to get messages or news out there.

"I'm working for the Fair and Square Repossession Company," Antar said, wincing, as if the job embarrassed him, "and I was the one to stumble across Sergeant Adams's body. All of his implants had been removed, not with any surgical precision. From the looks of it, he died as he was lunging out of bed. There was a tiny puncture wound in his neck. I'm assuming he was poisoned. Sir, I've done some research, and the others all died in similar manners. They were poisoned, or otherwise killed in their sleep, and then their implants were removed. The implants were all removed with a scalpel or a knife rather than a surgeon's laser cutter. At least one other man had a small puncture wound in his neck and poison was suspected. With the others, I bet the punctures were also there, but nobody noticed them." Antar grimaced again. "Or cared enough to look."

"Probably," Leonidas muttered, well aware of how most of the system felt about cyborgs. It had taken a while before Alisa had called him anything except "cyborg" or "mech," or had even asked for his name. Not that he'd put any effort into being approachable back then. She'd been wearing an Alliance flight jacket when they first met, and it had been too soon after the war for him to see her as anything other than an enemy.

"I'm afraid," Antar continued on, "that someone is targeting cyborgs—former Cyborg Corps cyborgs—so they can make money selling our implants on the black market, and that they have some way of sneaking up on us. I haven't kept in touch with many of the men since the war ended, and I didn't know who else to comm. And since it looks like they're going alphabetically, I wanted to warn you to watch your back because your name should already have come up on the list. Also, it seems like someone should do...*something*. The idea of our kind being hacked up for parts just so someone can make a profit is…" Antar spread his arms, no hint of the prankster in his glum, vulnerable expression. "Please let me know if you can help, sir. I'm still paying off my school loans, and I don't have a lot of resources right now, but this isn't right. I want to help make sure whoever this is can't just go down the roster and kill everyone in our old unit. I'm about to leave Targos Moon. If you want to meet somewhere—" Antar glanced to the side and lowered his voice. "Just let me know. I'm not sure if I can talk my pilot into letting me use this ship if there isn't a repo involved, but I'll do what I need to do to be there if you name a place. And if you can't help, at least let me know that you're alive, sir. Antar, out."

"Huh," Leonidas said and rubbed his chin.

"That's surprising," Alisa said.

"That some greedy person or entity would target cyborgs?"

"No, that they'd be successful doing it. You aren't that easy to kill."

"True," he murmured.

"And aren't there civilian cyborgs out there? Rich people who can afford the upgrades? You'd think they'd be easier targets than former soldiers from the Cyborg Corps."

Leonidas nodded, but he wasn't surprised that someone had chosen to go after men from his own unit—the Corps had killed a lot of rebels, as the people in the Alliance had been called then, before and during the war. Many of those people, people who had once been considered criminals, were now in charge of the system. If someone had concocted a safe way to kill cyborgs from a distance, then making money might only be part of the plot. Maybe that someone believed the time had come for revenge. Furthermore, the deaths of rich civilians who'd purchased upgrades would be investigated, especially if they were rich *Alliance* civilians. Who would bother investigating the deaths of cyborg soldiers from the losing side of the war?

Even though the reasoning was logical, Leonidas found himself clenching his jaw hard enough to hurt. *He* wasn't out seeking revenge on those who had destroyed his way of life and murdered the emperor and the emperor's wife simply to cement a victory. Surely, he'd have as much right for vengeful wishes—and actions—as anyone. But honorable men did not murder people, even those who might deserve it. And taking revenge on soldiers who had been following the orders of their superiors? That was *not* acceptable. Few of his cyborg soldiers had been angels, and some of them had liked the killing far more than they should have, but he'd made sure they followed their orders and nothing more, nothing criminal. As had those who had gone before him, damn it. The Corps had always acted with honor, and those who hadn't had been punished and dealt with. His people hadn't been among the war criminals tried after the war. There had been no need. It had been the leaders who'd occasionally committed atrocities. Not the cyborgs who worked for them.

"I can hear your teeth grinding from here," Alisa said. "We'll drop off our cargo tomorrow. Shall I make plans to fly you somewhere to meet him after that?"

Leonidas forced his jaw to unclench. He hadn't been excited to see Antar's face before, but now he *did* want to meet with him and do something about this. Badly. Adams had been a bit of an ass, someone who would have gotten himself killed eventually even if there wasn't a plot afoot, but Abadi and Albrecht had been good men. They weren't troublemakers. And he'd met Alvarado on Perun for drinks a couple of years earlier. Yes, he'd been one of those plotting to bring back the empire, but only because he'd been passionate. An idealist. He surely hadn't deserved to be murdered.

"Aren't we supposed to pick up a return cargo?" Leonidas asked, though he was already thinking of a logical place where he could ask Antar to meet them. Primus 7? If Antar was coming from Targos Moon, the station would not be far out of the way for either of them, and the casino-filled tourist trap would be a good place not to be noticed. "We're supposed to head to Indra next, aren't we?" he added.

"Yes, the *Nomad* is committed for the next four months, but the schedule is flexible enough that I can drop you off to give your friend some advice."

"My soldier," he said.

Leonidas barely knew Antar. The kid had been in Captain Song's company, too young and low-ranking to have much interaction with senior officers. If not for the whoopee cushion and the day Antar had come into his office, pleading to be released from the unit and medically discharged for "depression," Leonidas might not have remembered him at all. That still rankled, the idea of someone trying to get out of the contract he had knowingly signed, especially during the war, when the empire had needed its cyborg soldiers the most.

"Oh, I'm promoting him to your friend. You need more pranksters in your life."

A young cry of "*Jelena!*" came from the direction of the mess hall, Maya complaining about her current babysitter. It was a toss up as to whether the three-year-olds or the twelve-year-old was up to mischief.

"Are you sure?" Leonidas asked. "I feel I may already have enough slots allocated to pranksters."

"I'm sure."

CHAPTER FOUR

Jasim sent the comm request from his cabin on the *Interrogator*, nerves tangling in his belly. He wasn't sure why. Adler had already agreed to meet him on Primus 7, and to have a preliminary discussion as soon as they were close enough for live communications. With the station less than six hours away, the time was now. If Jasim should be nervous about dealing with anyone, it was Maddy.

He'd told her that his armor had taken more damage than expected during that rooftop battle and that he needed to stop and visit a reputable smith on Primus 7 before continuing on. Of course, his case had been able to repair the few scuffs his gear had taken, but he didn't think Maddy knew much about the various kinds of combat armor. Few people in the repo business could afford it. Maddy hadn't protested the stop too much, since she liked to gamble a touch here and there, but Jasim had no idea how she would react if he shared that he needed to take a trip across the system to find a murderer. He had no doubt that The Pulverizer had more assignments lined up for them. Unless he sent Adler off to deal with the murderer alone—which would hardly be the proper thing to do—he would have to figure out a way to take some time off work. The problem was The Pulverizer wasn't generous when it came to granting leave.

A face appeared in the holodisplay above his netdisc. Colonel Adler.

His hair had as much gray as it did black now, but it was still cut short, still very military. As was he. His jaw was shaven, his features sharp and lean, his blue eyes hard, and was that his old Cyborg Corps jacket he wore?

"Sir," Jasim said, sitting up straight in his chair. "Thank you for talking now and for agreeing to meet in person on the station."

Adler had sent a reply to Jasim's message four days earlier, but it had taken a while for them both to fly to Primus 7, the meeting spot Adler had suggested.

"I've sent you all the information I have," Jasim hurried on, knowing there would be a lag before Adler heard his message, and not wanting to confuse things with pauses. "And I imagine you've done some research of your own by now. I believe I have to go look for this killer in person. I would prefer not to go alone. Can you get away to come with me? Or can you at least suggest some resources that might help?"

Jasim could make use of McCall, if he could afford her, but finding the person or persons responsible for the cyborg deaths might only be part of the problem. Surely, someone who could kill their kind so easily was a dangerous foe—and would be prepared for retribution.

Adler's facial expression did not change as he listened to the words—nothing was coming as a surprise.

"I've done some research, yes," Adler said, "and I agree with your sentiment. This is a Corps problem, so the Corps must be the solution, whether or not it exists anymore outside of the memories of men. We need to find these people and handle them on our own. Even if we wished help from outsiders, it's unlikely that any civilian authorities currently in existence care about protecting our comrades. Or punishing those who are murdering them. Over."

"I agree, sir. It's horrible that someone is profiting from our deaths and that they needn't fear retribution. They must know they have nothing to worry about, at least from the authorities." Jasim vowed that there would be *another* sort of retribution, and that these people would die regretting their actions. "Whoever the greedy parties are, they need to be stopped."

"It may be more than greed motivating them," Adler said, "but we can start with sys-net research and try to figure out if used implants are flooding any particular world's black markets. Over."

"More than greed, sir?" Jasim thought of the expensive combat armor that had been left behind, but he had assumed that had been because some robot or drone hadn't been programmed to take it.

"As former imperial soldiers, we have a lot of enemies."

"I…see, sir. I have a research specialist contact who may be able to get more information. For a price." Jasim did not hint that he needed money from Adler—he had no idea how wealthy his former commander was these days—but it crossed his mind. Hiring McCall certainly would be easier if Adler could contribute some funds.

"Good, but there's going to be a limit to how much research can be done over the sys-net. And at some point, we'll have to go to confront the murderer." Adler's eyes closed to slits. "*Personally.*"

"Yes, sir. Agreed. I assumed we'd have to take a trip." Assumed, yes. Explained it to his pilot, no.

"My wife operates a freighter, but she has contracts she can't break away from, so we'll have to use commercial transport options," Adler said. "Unless you have a ship."

Hm, Jasim *sort of* had a ship. Normally, he wouldn't volunteer Maddy and the *Interrogator* for ferry duty, but if he could somehow get her to agree to it, to even back it…Her word would hold a lot more weight with The Pulverizer. Jasim might not be fired promptly for taking on this quest. Besides, he had a feeling their search might take them to places that weren't easily accessible by commercial transport. It would be far more convenient to have the use of a ship.

"I have a ship," Jasim said. He'd figure out how to explain it to Maddy later.

"Excellent. I'll be on Primus 7 in about eight hours. Coming in on the *Star Nomad.*"

"I'll see you there. I look forward to working with you, sir."

Adler grunted and cut the comm. Nerves tormented Jasim's stomach again. He had a feeling there were at least a hundred other cyborgs that Adler wished had reached out to him, and even though he barely knew his old commander, he couldn't help but feel disappointed that Adler didn't want to work with him.

"It's not important," Jasim told himself. "Finding the murderers is."

———

Leonidas removed neatly folded stacks of underwear and T-shirts from his clothes cabinet in the cabin he shared with Alisa and tucked them into his armor case. He turned back, reaching for the bin that held the sock squares the military had long ago trained him to make, but the bin was empty. He'd done the laundry himself, to make sure he would have what he needed, and he distinctly remembered putting away his socks.

"Someone is conspiring against me," he announced, looking toward the hatchway and holding out the empty bin for display.

Alisa had been alternating between watching the twins make towers out of condiment bottles in the mess hall and monitoring his packing progress, and she stood there now, her shoulder against the jamb.

"Hm," she said, arching an eyebrow. "Maybe I'm not the only one who doesn't want you to leave."

Leonidas blinked and lowered the bin. "You don't want me to leave? You volunteered to deviate from the *Nomad's* flight path to bring me to Primus 7."

"To meet and advise your soldier-friend, yes. At that time, I didn't realize you planned to go off to find and confront someone clever enough and strong enough to kill cyborgs." Alisa smiled faintly, though there was a wryness to the gesture. "I'm not sure *why* I didn't realize you'd insist on going along. I mean, I do know you fairly well at this point."

"There's nobody else who will handle this problem."

"Are you sure about that? Whether you want to admit it or not, you do know people high up in the Alliance. Some of them even like you."

"They like *Beck*," Leonidas said, waving toward the mess hall. Beck's catering gigs were infrequent, but after doing Senator Hawk's wedding, he tended to attract high-profile clients.

"Yes, but you impressively carried Beck's food trays at many of the parties he's worked. Therefore, they like you too. Who doesn't love the cyborg who brings in the brown-sugar-and-cinnamon grilled pineapples?" Alisa's smile faded. "I'm just saying that you could call in a few favors if you wanted."

"This is a Corps problem. More than that, I can't trust anyone else to want to help former imperial cyborg soldiers. I can't trust anyone else to *care*." Leonidas met her eyes. "I know you understand."

"I do," Alisa said, walking in to slip her arms around his waist. "I'm just concerned for you." She rested the side of her face against his shoulder.

"This isn't your typical pirate or smuggler plot. You know damn well how hard you are to kill. If someone has been successfully murdering your people…Well, it sounds like someone has figured out a super weapon."

"A super poison-delivery mechanism is more like it. I'll keep my armor on. Nothing is going to prick my neck through that." He wrapped one arm around her and patted the metal gorget in his armor case with his free hand.

Alisa's "Hm," did not sound convinced.

He did not dismiss her concerns, as he understood her point, but he'd walked into potentially deadly trouble countless times over the years, many of those times since he'd met her. Maybe she thought this would be different since she wouldn't be there to watch over him and contribute her schemes to whatever plans he came up with. There was a time when he would have allowed her to join him on such a mission…yes, even to help him, but that had been before Nika and Maya had been born, and before Jelena had come to live with them. Now it seemed more important that one of them stay safe, that one of them always be there for the children.

Of course, he fully intended to come back to them. He was still fit enough to handle these murderers; he was sure of it. And, he admitted silently, a part of him longed to once again feel adrenaline surging through his veins, to go out and make a difference in the system again. To matter to more than his family.

"Of course," he said gently, Alisa's grip around him still tight, "if I don't have any socks to wear, the villainous cowards might simply shoot poison at my toes."

"Uh huh. You don't wear socks when you're in your armor. You hardly wear anything. It's a good thing that box sanitizes everything so well." She wrinkled her nose and waved to his case.

"Still, I'm certain I'd fare better in battle if my feet had been properly warmed ahead of time."

"*I* didn't take them."

"I believe that, but I suspect you know the culprit. You may even be related to her."

Alisa sighed and stepped back, lowering her arms. She leaned out into the corridor. "Jelena, have you seen Leonidas's socks?"

There was a long pause before the words, "Define *seen*," came from a nearby cabin.

"With your eyeballs or with your telepathic mind's eye. Or with the chickens' eyes. Or the geese's. Or anyone else's on the ship."

"That's quite a broad definition of the word," Leonidas murmured.

"Just trying to head off obfuscation."

Jelena appeared in the hatchway, her arms full of familiar folded sock squares. She gave Alisa a sulky look. "You weren't supposed to help him find them. Or tattle on your daughter."

"He needs them for his trip."

"But you don't want him to go." Jelena pushed her braid over her shoulder, dropping a couple of sock pairs in the process. "I could tell. And nobody goes on a trip without socks. Or underwear. I thought about taking his underwear, too, but, ew, gross."

Leonidas thought to protest this malign of his underwear, but Alisa spoke first.

"I don't *not* want him to go on his trip, especially when I'm sure he's looking forward to it." She gave him a pointed look, and he almost suspected her of the same telepathy her daughter possessed. "I just want him to be safe and come back to me with all of his pieces still attached."

Jelena looked a little confused, but she came in and dropped the socks in the bin. Then she hugged Leonidas. "Don't get killed, Dad. Or lose pieces."

"It would never occur to me to allow either." Leonidas patted her on the back. "Your mother would be extremely peeved if I did."

"*Extremely*," Alisa agreed.

A squeal came from the mess hall.

"Will you go check on that, please, Jelena?" Alisa asked.

Jelena released Leonidas from her hug. "So you can get me out of the cabin so you two can smooch?"

"Not *only* so we can smooch."

Jelena rolled her eyes but jogged out to check on the twins.

Alisa picked up the abandoned socks on the deck and walked them over to Leonidas. "What would you say to taking my father along with you? Those murderers may have plans in place to deal with cyborgs, but I bet a Starseer would be unanticipated and throw a wrench in the works."

It wasn't a bad idea, one that Leonidas might have considered, but…

"I don't know how long this will take," he said. "I don't want you out there, possibly running into pirates, without anyone besides Beck for protection."

"Beck and *me*," she said pointedly, waving to the blue case that held her own armor. "And don't forget Jelena and the goose army."

Leonidas smiled. "I know you're a capable warrior, as are the geese, but Stanislav is a trump card, and it's more important that you have him." She opened her mouth, the protest clearly coming, and he added, "You and the children."

Her mouth shut. No matter how much she wanted to argue with him, she knew he was right, that the safety of the children had to be paramount over all.

"All right, but if you don't come back to me, I'll give Jelena your share in the company, and she'll insist on turning this into an all-animal-all-the-time freighter outfit. Donkeys and goats and who knows what else will probably roam freely through the corridors and eat all of our socks."

"That does sound horrific."

"Very horrific."

Leonidas stepped forward, pulling her into a hug again, this time delivering a long kiss as well.

When he eventually drew back, he murmured, "I'll be careful. I love you."

"And I love you. Much more than I love donkeys."

"You're still an odd woman, Captain Marchenko."

"And you're damn lucky to have me."

"Yes. I am."

Thunderous footfalls sounded in the corridor. It was amazing that such lightweight individuals could run so loudly.

Nika burst into the cabin first, carrying a couple of toys and jumping the small lip of the hatchway like a track sprinter. Maya, her arms so full of stuffed animals that she could barely see, tripped over the lip and splatted onto the deck. Leonidas rushed forward and picked her up.

"What's all this?" he hurried to ask, since Maya wore a distinctly familiar expression, one that said she wasn't hurt but that she was still contemplating bursting into tears, because it seemed the right thing to do after a fall.

"We came to help you pack," Nika said brightly. "This is for you." She thrust up her plush, musical-planets toy, Aldrin's moons jangling with internal bells.

"And Mister Cow and Stumpy Snagor." Maya pointed to the fallen stuffed animals from her spot in his arms. "And Brother Bear. And do you want my blankie? It's scary to go away from the ship without a blankie."

"It is indeed," Leonidas murmured, not certain what to say as Nika grabbed a couple of the stuffed animals, in addition to the planets toy, and walked over and peered into his armor case.

"There aren't any paints or blocks," Nika said sternly, frowning up at him, as if she couldn't imagine battling villains without such staples.

Alisa swatted Leonidas on the arm. "What were you thinking? Worrying about socks when the paints and blocks weren't in your kit yet?"

"I...don't know," he said, watching Nika place the toys atop his T-shirts.

"Let me get my blankie," Maya said, and squirmed to be let down.

"Don't you think you'll need it while I'm gone?" Leonidas asked.

"I want you to have it, Daddy." Maya rushed out, almost tripping again in her haste.

"Uhm," Leonidas said, as Nika grabbed more stuffed animals and placed them in the case. Well, not *in* it, since the items were piling up to the point where he couldn't have closed the lid, even if he wanted to take all those items.

He looked to Alisa, not sure if he should stop this familial packing help, or simply wait until they finished and left, and then hide the items in a cabinet in here. She was watching, her fist to her lips, her eyes twinkling. She didn't offer him an iota of assistance.

"Here it is," Maya ran in with her purple Andromeda Android blanket dangling from one hand, the end dragging on the deck. Impressively, she managed to enter without tripping over the blanket or the hatchway lip. It went into the armor case atop the stuffed animals.

Leonidas cleared his throat. "Thank you, girls. I think I can handle the rest of the packing on my own."

"Welcome," they blurted together and ran over, each hugging one of his legs.

Leonidas dropped a hand to each of their heads.

"All right," Alisa said, waving the girls toward the hatchway. "Let's give your dad a few minutes of peace to finish. Do I smell cookies in the oven?"

"Brownies," Nika blurted and raced into the corridor. "Uncle Tommy's making brownies."

Maya made excited cooing noises and followed.

Alisa waited until they were gone to say, "Be careful, Leonidas. I know you can handle a lot, but it doesn't reassure me that there's someone out there with a list of cyborgs, and you're overdue for a visit."

"Precisely why I intend to visit that someone first."

"All right." She smiled, though it appeared forced, and headed out of the cabin. She paused in the hatchway to look back one more time. "Don't forget to pack your paints and blocks."

Leonidas had been thinking more along the lines of blazer rifles and grenade launchers, but he bowed obediently.

"And to come back to me," she added softly before disappearing into the corridor.

CHAPTER FIVE

Jasim smoothed a hand down his black shirt and made sure it was tucked in. As he waited in the busy commercial airlock area at Primus 7, it occurred to him that he should have cut his hair. Would the colonel scowl at its non-regulation length? They were both years out of the fleet, so Adler couldn't possibly expect that Jasim would look like a soldier anymore, but one never knew with career officers, even former career officers. They could be sticklers for…everything.

A boxy gray freighter appeared outside the expansive portholes in front of Airlock 73, maneuvering to come in between two smaller, far more elegant ships in the adjoining locks. It looked older than the original colony ships. Not exactly the luxurious—or at least modern—ship one might expect a former high-ranking officer to have. Jasim's hopes that Adler might have money to pay McCall faded. But what had he expected? He hadn't heard of many high-ranking imperial officers who had come out of the war with great wealth and influence. Most of them had been lucky not to be shot during the Masterson War Crimes Trials. Those who had come out with money and power…were suspicious. There had been a lot of double-crosses at the end of the war. Jasim decided it was a good thing that Colonel Adler was traveling on an inauspicious old freighter. Maybe the cyborg murderer, as Jasim had come to think of their unidentified foe, hadn't found Adler because of his unlikely conveyance.

To his surprise, the freighter did a lazy barrel roll before extending its tube and securing it to the lock. Jasim was probably the only one who noticed. People from all walks of life pushed past him with bulging shopping bags and cups full of casino chips. The airlock was across a wide promenade from a casino, a brothel, and an all-you-can-eat buffet—he had visited the latter while waiting, having little interest in the former two offerings.

Maddy was back on the ship, which had a spot at Airlock 14, waiting for him to get his armor fixed. He'd thought about explaining everything to her, but he doubted she would care about dead cyborgs. Further, The Pulverizer might consider it a liability if one of his workers had a target on his back. Even if this wasn't Jasim's dream job, it paid well, especially when bonuses were included, and he was getting close to having his university loan paid off. He had certainly worked worse jobs with less freedom since the end of the war.

Jasim avoided the bustling people while keeping an eye on them as he headed toward Airlock 73. Typically, he wouldn't worry about being harassed by thieves or muggers. Even if being just under six feet tall had made him short for the Cyborg Corps, he still had the thickly muscled body of one of the empire's creations. Today, however, he watched people with more wariness than usual, well aware that his surname made him one of the next targets on the roster, if not *the* next one. He picked out a couple of androids among the crowd, well aware that their power matched his. If one got close enough with a syringe, and Jasim wasn't paying attention, it could deliver a deadly dose.

The airlock hatch opened, and Jasim walked close enough to peer through the attached tube. Voices from inside reached his sensitive ears, but none of them sounded like Adler. He supposed he should wait where he was, but he preferred to get away from the busy promenade. There weren't any walls or posts that he could lean against, and his shoulder blades itched. Besides, Adler was expecting him, right?

Jasim walked down the tube, through an open airlock chamber, and poked his head into a voluminous cargo hold. Someone in gray and white combat armor stood nearby, leaning against a stack of crates. That wasn't the colonel, not unless he'd lost his red gear and had to buy a civilian set. But no, the man had his helmet off, and Jasim didn't recognize him. Some small animal—was that a chicken?—tried to trundle toward the open airlock hatch, but the man picked it up and strode toward a coop full of squawking chickens and an unorthodox aquaponics tank that looked almost like a pond. Fake grass covered the deck around it—or maybe that *wasn't* fake grass. Ducks and geese trundled around the area, plucking at who knew what.

He supposed freighters hauled all manner of cargo. Still, he wondered if he was poking his head into the wrong ship. Adler had said he'd arrive on a freighter called the *Star Nomad*, and Jasim had looked it up and seen it assigned to 73, but this seemed a strange place to find a former imperial fleet colonel.

Jasim cleared his throat, wondering if he should call out his presence or simply wait for Adler to show up. The man in combat armor had disappeared from sight behind the stacks of magnetic crates fastened to the deck and hull. Jasim could still hear him walking around back there. Perhaps seeking another escaped chicken?

"Hello?" Jasim called.

"Here, here!" came an enthusiastic young cry from a walkway above the cargo hold. A little girl of three or four ran out a doorway and into sight, her dark brown pigtails dancing.

"Me too," another young voice yelled, and a very similar-looking girl, this one with her hair up in a flip-flopping knot, charged out.

"You girls aren't going anywhere," said the man behind the crates. "This is a space station, not a place to ride horses."

He strode into view, this time holding two chickens. He headed toward the coop, or maybe the stairs to the walkway, so he could block the exit. Those determined kids hadn't slowed down at all.

A tall, broad-shouldered man strode out onto the walkway after the children, and Jasim, who had once again been wondering if he had the right place, snapped to attention, his heels clicking together. Colonel Adler still appeared every bit the cyborg soldier, even if he wore khaki trousers and a brown snagor-hide jacket instead of a uniform. He didn't look like he'd lost any muscle—or any of his ability to kill people.

The children only made it down two stairs before he swooped them up, one in each arm.

"Nooo," one protested, an arm stretching toward the open hatch.

"Foiled," the second one said. "Rats!"

Adler, his hands full, nodded once toward Jasim, as if he'd known he was there all along. Maybe he'd heard that hello.

The armored man stopped at the bottom of the stairs and looked up at the colonel. "Does it bother you that she's quoting the mad scientist villain from the cartoon instead of the hero?"

"No," Adler said. "Does it bother you that you're wrangling chickens?"

"Not anymore, no. Yumi has me trained."

"I think she has us all trained." Adler looked back along the walkway toward the corridor.

Jasim heard someone else's footsteps before the person appeared, an attractive woman in her mid-thirties. She smiled at Adler or perhaps at the children, and her eyes gleamed with good humor. Somehow, Jasim suspected that the kids plotting escapes was not uncommon.

"I believe these are staying with you," Adler said, turning toward her with his cargo.

One of the girls stuck a finger in his ear and giggled. He removed it, gave her a stern look, and murmured something. She nodded solemnly, but as soon as he looked away, the finger went back in his ear.

Jasim realized his mouth was hanging open and shut it. The whole situation stunned him. He'd never seen Adler with children and had somehow assumed they would be as terrified of him as all of the lower enlisted soldiers were. Hells, he'd never seen *any* of the cyborgs with children. It wasn't as if they could have any of their own. Unfortunately. Knowing that was part of what had drawn Jasim to get a degree in education. He'd imagined himself coaching or teaching children, even if he couldn't have his own. He'd also thought that maybe, even if he couldn't make up for all those he'd killed during the war, helping young people might be a way to do something good going forward. He would have loved it if a friendly soldier had taken him under his arm when he'd been a kid. Maybe then, he would have known what to do when the gangs came for his sisters.

"Yes," the woman said, coming close enough to rest her hands on Adler's chest. "We'll miss you."

She kissed him on the mouth, and Jasim's thoughts of his past fled. He nearly fell over. Especially when Adler seemed to return the kiss. It was hard to tell around the children's heads, but yes, that was definitely a kiss.

They didn't hold it overly long, but Jasim could only stare, stunned. Adler couldn't have gotten anything out of that, could he? And—by the holy Suns Trinity—those couldn't be *his* children, could they? How could that be possible? Hadn't he had the same surgery that Jasim had undergone? That *all* the imperial cyborgs had undergone?

Adler handed the children to the woman, who lowered them to the walkway and clasped their hands. She looked down to Jasim, gave him a quick smile, then turned a slightly worried look back onto Adler.

"Are you sure you don't want my father to go with you?" she asked.

Adler shook his head. "Yes, I'm sure, and I already told you why. Besides, whatever this is, I doubt it's Starseer business."

Jasim stared. Starseers?

He looked uneasily around the cargo hold. There wasn't one *here*, was there? All he saw was the armored man returning those two chickens to their fenced-in area, but who knew what the rest of the ship held?

"I know that—though some of them want you cyborgs dead, too, you know," the woman said.

"Most of them, I'd imagine. But they wouldn't use poison to kill us. They would diddle with our minds." Adler tapped a finger to his temple.

"Probably. But Stan would go along just to help you. I'm sure he doesn't want me to become a single mother again."

"I don't want that either." He leaned close and kissed her on the cheek. "But I also don't want to deprive you of your security on the next leg of your journey."

The man by the chicken coop cleared his throat loudly and tapped a fist against his chest piece. "Did we forget that I am the *original* security officer around here?"

"Beck, you're too busy cooking to notice when pirates are invading the ship," the woman said, "and you know it."

"I notice them," the man—Beck—protested. "I just wait to see if Leonidas and Stanislav are going to handle things before I go for my weapons."

"Go get your groceries," the woman said, shooing him toward the airlock hatch where Jasim stood. "And don't get yourself shot at. You seem to be dressed for trouble rather than a shopping trip."

"You never know what you'll find on a station full of drunks, Captain. I like to be prepared. Besides, I can lift more groceries in my armor." Beck pretended to flex his biceps.

Adler touched the woman's face and headed down the stairs. "Oh," he said, halfway down, looking at Jasim. "Introductions. Corporal Antar, this is the captain of the *Star Nomad* and my wife, Alisa Marchenko. Alisa, Corporal Antar, formerly of Bravo Company."

Wife?

Jasim didn't want to ask how that could be—corporals, even former corporals, didn't ask their commanding officers about their personal lives—but he couldn't help but wonder. And an inkling that he should feel betrayed came to mind. Had some cyborgs *not* had to undergo that aspect of the surgery?

"Ask him for his doctor's card," Beck said, smirking at Jasim as he walked into the airlock tube with an empty hoverboard turned on its side and trailing after him.

"I...ah..." Jasim cleared his throat. This wasn't why he had come, and it didn't matter, not when cyborgs were being killed. "You can call me Jasim, ma'am," he told Adler's wife. "And, ah, you can too...sir." He looked at Adler, not sure if that would be awkward or inappropriate, but neither of them were soldiers anymore. They were civilians. Just people.

"Mm," was all Adler said.

He waved to his wife—Alisa—and headed over to join Jasim. Jasim tried not to feel scrawny with him standing more than six inches taller than he. *He* hadn't struggled to meet height requirements at any point in his life.

"Is my armor case coming?" Adler called back toward the walkway.

His wife smirked, and started toward the corridor with the two little girls ambling to either side of her. A few seconds passed, and a tall, gangly girl with her brown hair back in a braid led a red armor case down the walkway, whistling, or trying to. Her grin must have made it hard to blow properly. Alisa and the little ones stood aside to allow the girl and the case floating after her to pass.

"She offered to get it for me," Adler told Jasim. "I suspect foul play."

"Sir?" Jasim asked, not comfortable calling him anything else unless invited to do so.

The girl reached the stairs leading down from the walkway and hopped onto the armor case, sitting cross-legged. It bobbed under her weight, but soon leveled back to its typical hover height, a few inches off the deck. Then, seemingly of its own accord, it zipped down the stairs, like a sled cruising down a snowy hill. The girl's grin widened as she rode it down, then leaned right and left to take advantage of the momentum and zipped around the cargo hold. She missed the stack of crates by inches before the case slowed to a stop next to Adler.

She hopped off, saying, "Here it is."

She tilted her head to look at Jasim, smiled shyly, and waved. Was this one Adler's child too? She was tall and lanky, and after that display, he wagered she would be good at sports.

"What is this?" Adler asked.

Jasim snapped his hand down. Maybe the colonel didn't want strange men waving at his daughter.

But he was looking at the armor case, not Jasim, and pointing to one of several decals and stickers adorning the outside. Their presence surprised Jasim, both because they were childish—he was pointing at a pink horse—and because there were regulations about keeping one's armor and case in pristine condition. Decorations weren't allowed. Even if the empire that had made those regulations was gone, it was hard to imagine Adler breaking the rules.

"That's a sticker," the girl said blandly.

"It's a *fifth* sticker," Adler said sternly, though he didn't truly sound very threatening. Jasim had heard him using his no-nonsense command tone, the one that could make grown men trip over themselves in their haste to obey. This wasn't it. "The deal is four on the case and two on the armor. *Max.*"

"Maya and Nika were afraid one might fall off while you're on your journey."

Some of the sternness, which seemed to be mock sternness anyway, faded. "Ah."

"I kept them from putting a whole *sheet* of stickers on," the girl said. "You should thank me."

"We'll see." He eyed his case as if it might contain booby traps. "Antar, this is Jelena, my wife's daughter. Jelena, Antar—Jasim."

"Hi, Jasim." She waved shyly again, then hugged Adler. "Mom is worried about you going off after a cyborg murderer."

"I know." Adler returned the hug. "Take care of her, all right?"

"Of course." Jelena waved to both of them the second time, then ran toward the back of the cargo hold. "Erick, Mom said to refuel the tanks. We're only staying here long enough for Uncle Tommy to shop."

Adler turned to face Jasim. "Have you heard anything new?"

"No, sir."

"Alvarado died on Perun, Albrecht on Demeter, Adams on Targos, and Abadi on Starfall Station, right?" Adler asked. "So our murderer or *murderers* are willing to travel, or send minions to travel for them, and seem more interested in going down the roster in alphabetical order than in batch processing targets."

Jasim grimaced at the idea of his former colleagues being "batch processed," but said, "Yes, sir. It's surprising they skipped you and moved on to the next one."

"We've been out near the Trajean Asteroid Belt, and we're not in the habit of announcing our routes or destinations to the entire system," Adler said.

"That's fortunate for you then. I've realized that I'm next on the list. I've thought about being open with my travel plans and then staying awake through the nights to try to catch whatever form of attack comes through the door. I don't sleep much anyway."

Adler's stern face softened slightly. "Nightmares?" he asked.

"Yeah." Jasim wasn't surprised he knew. Most of the men had suffered from them to some extent or another, whether they were remorseless killing machines or not. He'd never known if they were a side effect of the surgeries or just a result of the work the cyborgs did. "I've alarmed a few of my pilots by banging on the walls in my sleep. Maddy—the pilot of my employer's ship—pretends she sleeps up in NavCom so she can keep an eye on things, but it may just be because her cabin is next to mine." Jasim forced a smile, even if the subject was not an amusing one. He suspected Adler remembered him as a whiner, if he remembered Jasim at all. Either way, he hoped to show that he'd changed. He'd been in a rough place mentally that first year of the war, but he'd like to think that he'd grown up since then, learned to take responsibility for his choices. He had no idea how to show Adler that. Funny that it even mattered all these years later.

"I've disturbed my pilot too," Adler said wryly. "The surgery helped a bit, and I can give you Dr. Tiang's contact information if you want to look him up on Arkadius, but my children's tutor, Yumi, was the one to find a weird little headband for me. It monitors my dreams, and if they turn distressing, it kicks me into another sleep cycle to end them."

"That sounds wonderful." Jasim pushed aside the comment about a surgery—what surgery?—and fixated on the rest of his words. Why hadn't he ever thought to look for such a thing?

"Sort of. It's a bit like this all night." Adler poked Jasim in the shoulder rhythmically several times. "But it lets me sleep with my wife without worrying about…worrying." He must not have wanted to talk about the details of that, because he quickly went on to say, "She wanted me to invite you to dinner when this is all done." His eyes narrowed to slits, as if he did not agree with the notion.

"Really? Because we're former, ah—" Jasim stopped himself, not wanting to presume to call them peers or colleagues, especially when he detected a hint of disapproval emanating from Adler. "Because we were in the same battalion?"

"Because I mentioned your propensity for whoopee cushions," Adler said.

"Oh." Heat flushed Jasim's cheeks. He'd hoped the colonel had forgotten about that incident, along with that day Jasim had gone to his office, asking to be discharged.

The blue earstar that Jasim wore draped over his right ear beeped softly, alerting him to a message. He almost ignored it so he wouldn't make the colonel wait, but the device deemed it a priority and projected a holo to the side of his eyes. He skimmed it quickly.

"Er, this is actually about the murders," he said, pointing to it. "Or I assume it is."

Adler nodded. "Take it."

"Answer," Jasim murmured, and Arlen McCall's tangled brown hair and freckled face appeared on the floating display. She always looked like she'd just gotten out of bed. "Did you comm to tell me how much I owe you for the cyborg information?" Jasim asked. It was a live transmission with little lag—McCall must have flown away from Bronos Moon to some nearby destination.

She blinked. "No, that was just a matter of looking at some news feeds. If you feel grateful, you can bring Meathead a bone sometime."

"I didn't think you allowed people on your ship."

"Not many," she agreed. "You can leave the bone outside of the hatch."

"Gotcha."

"I commed because someone offered me a job, not one of my usual clients."

"Oh?" Jasim asked, assuming this had something to do with him. She wasn't in the habit of discussing clients with him.

"The person wanted to know where Colonel Hieronymus Adler is. I thought it was odd that someone *else* was looking for him this week."

Jasim looked over the top of McCall's floating head to meet Adler's sharp blue eyes. His ears were as enhanced as Jasim's, so he must have heard that.

"Yes," Jasim said. "Did you tell this person where to find him? And do you know who this person *is*?"

"I told him or her or them—the message was text-based and routed through different nodes to keep the sender's identity and location secret—I'd think about accepting the assignment. They weren't offering a great many tindarks, and I'm not eager to piss off cyborgs, especially those with connections to powerful government officials on both sides."

Both sides? Alliance and empire? Who did Adler know in the Alliance? Jasim looked at him again, but his face didn't give anything away.

"Who is this?" Adler asked quietly, waving at the holodisplay.

"A skip tracer. She can find anyone."

"If you bribe her dog with bones?"

"She likes money too."

McCall snorted. "Just gotta make enough to pay my taxes, like anyone else."

"I've seen your ship," Jasim said. "It's new and nice and fast enough for the Tri-Suns races." He could only dream of having enough money to buy his own ship. He would settle for a job that made him proud to wake up and go to work each morning.

"When you're hunting down dangerous people and pointing them out to even more dangerous people, it's always useful to be able to run away afterward. You want to make a counteroffer on this?"

"Yes," Adler said before Jasim could ask what she meant. "How much does she want to look up the party who tried to hire her?"

"She said they hid themselves."

"And you just said she could find anyone."

"McCall?" Jasim asked. "Did you hear that? Can you—"

"Of course, I can. And I already did, because I don't like working for anonymous anyones. I could share the information for—how much do you make in that repo gig?"

"Not much."

"All right. Five hundred tindarks."

"You get paid that much to sit in a room and look things up?" Jasim asked, gaping.

"Actually, I'm giving you a discount because we've done business together before."

"We agree to the amount," Adler said before Jasim could do the math and figure out if he could make his loan payment this month if he took out that much. Maybe his wife's freight business did better than the aged ship implied.

"The person who wanted to hire me is Terrance Dufour," McCall said. "There's no home address registered anywhere, but he gets his mail on Dustor. I can't promise you he gets it *often*, but it should be a starting point."

"I understand," Jasim said. It was just like any other gig. He might have to ask around and bribe some people—or use some force—to find the target's ultimate location. "Out of curiosity, how much did he offer for the colonel's information?"

"A thousand," McCall said. "Don't forget to send bones. Meathead likes bacon too."

She cut the comm.

"Looks like we're going to Dustor, sir," Jasim said.

"My favorite place," Adler said, his tone making it clear that it wasn't.

No, Dustor wasn't *anyone's* favorite place. Jasim doubted even the crime lords and mafia thugs who ran the sandy desert planet liked it.

"You said you have transportation?" Adler asked. "My wife needs to deliver her next cargo."

He looked toward the room Jelena had disappeared into—engineering? Soft bawks came from beyond the hatchway. Were there *more* chickens back there? The ones in the coop squawked in response.

A young man in a black robe walked into view, a netdisc in his hand, a tool belt at his waist, and a dozen chickens following him along as if they were sheep and he the shepherd.

"Is that a *Starseer* robe?" Jasim asked, remembering the offhand comment from earlier.

"Yes." Adler nodded at the young man, but tapped his armor case, then pointed toward the airlock tube. As he headed into it, ushering Jasim ahead of him, his case—and its five stickers—floated after them. "Where's your ship?"

"Down that way," Jasim said as they came out of the airlock and into the crowded promenade. He pointed past a couple dozen casinos and hundreds of people. "But it's not technically mine, and the pilot may need to be convinced that it's a good idea to make a side trip to Dustor. As far as I know, we don't have anything that needs to be picked up there."

"Convinced with force or money?" Adler asked as they walked into the crowds.

"I wouldn't recommend force. Money, maybe. But actually…yes, I saw a booth on the way over here. Follow me, sir. I have an idea."

CHAPTER SIX

"How much for that shimmery rainbow string?" Jasim asked, pointing toward the back of the booth and pretending he couldn't feel Adler's eyes upon him, wondering why they had stopped to shop.

"*String?*" The tattooed woman manning the booth propped a fist on her hip. "If you don't know that it's called yarn, then let me direct you to an already finished product. How about a nice beanie for you or your hulking friend? It can get nippy out there in space."

Adler faced the promenade and the people walking by rather than the booth, but he did glance back for this comment.

"I don't think he's the type to wear a beanie," Jasim said. "He likes getting nipped."

"Only by my wife," Adler murmured.

Jasim hadn't meant to make a joke and didn't know how to respond to that. He turned back to the shopkeeper. "What I'm interested in is your yarn. It's for a friend who knits." A friend he needed to bribe.

The woman grumbled but reached for the yarn he'd pointing out. "Do you want a hank, skein, or shall I wind it into a center-pull ball?"

"Uhm, yes?"

She rolled her eyes at him.

Adler slapped him on the back. Jasim thought it might have to do with his knitting ignorance, but he tilted his chin toward a group of men in black snagor-hide jackets riding black thrust bikes down the middle of the promenade. Was that allowed on a space station? Granted, the promenade and locks area was wider than most sports fields and several stories tall, but most people were walking or using the moving sidewalks rather than riding vehicles. The men on the bikes were looking directly at Adler, scarcely noticing when they bumped into people, or knocked them over.

"I'll take one of each of those," Jasim said, pointing quickly at a couple of types of yarn, "and some of those there too. Wrap them up nice, please. They're a present." He eyed the approaching bikers, hoping Adler was just being careful and the gang wouldn't be a threat to either of them.

"Such a polite hulk," the woman muttered, grabbing more bunches of yarn from her display.

"How reliable is your skip tracer?" Adler asked as the thrust-bike riders continued toward them. He pushed his armor case toward the canvas wall of the booth where it would be out of the way. If those men had trouble on their minds, there wouldn't be time for him to don his armor.

"She's always dealt straight with me," Jasim said, "but my boss is usually the one paying her, and he's not someone you betray."

"Are you?"

"I hope not," Jasim said before realizing that didn't sound very tough. He supposed this wasn't the right time to mention his degree in education and that he had never intended to become a professional thug, that he was only working for The Pulverizer because nobody would hire a cyborg to be anything that didn't involve pulping, or outright killing people. Nobody had laughed in his face when he'd applied for teaching positions, but there had been a lot of startled and concerned looks prior to the rejections.

The group of bike riders pulled up in front of the yarn booth, revving their engines. There were eight of them, all men, except for one in the back with long hair and voluptuous curves. Though she was dressed similarly to the men, her skin didn't look quite real, and she had the silvery eyes typical of androids. That likely made her more dangerous than the men, even if she wasn't a combat model.

"Your kind aren't welcome here," a burly, mustached man said, taking a hand off the handlebars to draw a sawed-off blazer rifle from a side holster.

Jasim was *positive* weapons weren't allowed on the station. It was a tourist mecca, after all. Where were the enforcers or whatever this place had when one needed them? Surely, there had to be security cameras in all the casinos. But he supposed whoever watched over those cameras wouldn't care about altercations taking place *outside* of their establishments.

"Primus 7 is a neutral station," Jasim said. "Anyone's welcome, or so the greeting transmission says when you fly in."

"Mechs aren't *anyones*," the man said, smirking at his wit.

All Adler did was stare at the biker, his eyes cold, but his relaxed stance supremely unconcerned. Jasim wouldn't normally be concerned about this group, either, but if the android jumped into a fight, she could balance the scales against him and Adler. There was also the possibility that these men had been sent as a diversion or to get them in trouble, perhaps detained in the station jail. What if McCall *had* sold the information on their whereabouts, and what if that Terrance person and his poison needles lurked nearby even now? Or was waiting at the jail facility?

Adler was positioned so he could see up and down the promenade while keeping their visitors in sight—maybe he, too, was thinking this might be a setup. Jasim stepped up beside him, puffing his chest out and flexing his shoulders. These fools had to know they would get hurt if they picked this fight.

"What's the matter, old man?" the leader asked, his finger massaging the trigger of his shotgun. "Your tongue not as muscled up as the rest of you?"

"*Old?*" Adler asked, his eyes narrowing.

"Back to back?" Jasim murmured, judging a fight inevitable. He also judged it inevitable that the smug leader would walk away from Adler with at least some of his teeth missing.

"Surround them," Adler said out of the side of his mouth.

"Just the two of us?"

More of the men were reaching for weapons. Shoppers and casino-goers took a wide berth around the burgeoning confrontation. Some turned back the way they had come. Jasim didn't see anyone running off like they intended to call security.

Jasim leaned forward, deciding that he and Adler should attack first, before the bikers were ready.

"Don't pull a weapon," Adler murmured, "and make sure they're down or fleeing before that spy box reports to the local enforcers."

Spy box? Shit, Jasim hadn't even seen it. Where was it?

He followed Adler's quick glance. Ah, it was in the shadows between two booths and not painted in the cold black the empire had used for the spy boxes that floated all over its cities, recording footage and reporting trouble. This one blended into the gray surroundings of the station. He hoped it was reporting the situation to station security now, and that numerous competent and well-armed people were on their way.

The leader looked at the spy box, too, but his smirk only deepened.

"*Now*," he told his men and jerked his blazer up, pointing it at Adler's chest.

He fired without hesitation, but Adler moved too quickly. The crimson energy bolt streaked through the air where he'd been standing and pierced the sides of the canvas yarn booth.

Jasim only hesitated long enough to push the shopkeeper, who was cursing instead of screaming or crying, down to the ground behind a trunk. Then he ran around the outside of the group, in case Adler had been serious about wanting them surrounded and also because that android in the back would be the more dangerous foe.

He grabbed one man's blazer on the way and threw his elbow into another, striking him hard enough to knock him off his bike. The one who'd tried to shoot Adler was already flying across the promenade as his bike skidded away in the opposite direction. Blazer bolts flew as the bikers fired wantonly, whether they had a target or not. People shouted and scattered as the fight began in earnest. Someone hollered, "Security, security!"

Too late now.

The android female spotted Jasim coming and sprang off her bike toward him. He dodged, but with her machine-given power and speed, she moved as rapidly as he did. Her fist clipped the side of his jaw, and even that glancing blow would have sent him spinning, bones breaking if he'd been a mere man. But his sturdy jaw accepted the blow, even if pain lanced through his skull from it. He lunged in closer instead of reeling away.

He pummeled her abdomen, driving her back against her bike. It was like punching a wall, a wall that hit back. Her hand snapped up, and she reached for his face, fingers curling like talons. He whipped up a block, deflecting the grab, and slammed his forehead into her face. Synthetic cartilage crunched under the blow, and she tumbled backward, falling over the bike.

Before he could feel any satisfaction, something slammed into his back, and something electrical zapped him, charging up and down his veins and rousing pain in every part of his body. Gasping, he almost tumbled over the bike after the android. He managed to brace himself and whirl around as a man wheeled his bike back toward him and swung his shock staff for a second time. This time, Jasim ducked the blow, coming up after the weapon swept over his head, ruffling his hair. He punched the wielder in the side of the face. The man dropped the staff as he flew backward, landing on his ass and skidding several feet to crash into a potted tree. It wobbled in its planter, then tipped over.

Jasim grabbed the staff and thought about lunging after the biker and using it on him, but the man was already out cold. Besides, Adler had said not to draw a weapon. Aware of the spy box recording footage, he snapped the staff over his knee instead, and hurled it onto the top of a booth dozens of meters away.

A roar sounded to his side. He spun, expecting to see another biker bearing down on him. To his surprise, Adler had claimed one of the thrust bikes. He stood astride it, weaving through the skirmish as he punched opponents or simply knocked them away. His eyes gleamed, as if he was enjoying the hells out of this fight.

Something zipped in toward Adler from the side, a two-foot-wide spherical bronze object. Not an object. A *drone*.

"Look out, sir!" Jasim warned.

He stepped forward, intending to intercept it, but the android jumped to her feet. Cursing, Jasim leaped over her bike and grabbed her. Before she could fully reboot her wits, he threw her across the promenade, into one of the massive pylons supporting the roof. She crashed into it, bounced off, and dropped onto the kiosk of a robot vender selling sausages on sticks. The robot did not bat an electronic eye, merely continued lifting its wares into the air and calling out the specials. Atop the now-dented kiosk, the android's boot twitched. The rest of her did not move, so Jasim hoped she was out of commission.

He whirled back toward the skirmish, looking for the bronze sphere and expecting more opponents to leap toward him at any second. He didn't see the drone. The bikers were all unconscious or groaning on the floor.

Several weapons lay bent and broken among them. Jasim didn't think any of the men were dead, and he was glad for that, even if they'd wanted to rid the station of cyborgs. He had never believed his commander, as aloof as Adler was, to be one of those men who enjoyed killing and gleefully did it whether required or not. He was glad to have the notion reaffirmed.

Adler was looking toward a kiosk next to the yarn booth. He stopped the bike he'd taken and hopped off. Blood trickled from a gouge in his jaw, but he did not otherwise appear injured. Jasim started to ask what they should do next, as he worried there would be repercussions for successfully defending themselves, but Leonidas turned his back on him and walked toward that kiosk. The drone, now severely dented, lay next to it.

He started forward, wanting a look, but stopped because two more thrust bikes were heading their way, these painted silver and blue. The two androids riding them wore uniforms that Jasim recognized: the station security enforcers.

Adler picked up the drone gingerly, using only his fingertips. He turned slowly, looking all around the promenade with narrowed eyes as he held the thing.

"What is it?" Jasim asked, keeping an eye on the androids but moving closer to Adler. Unease crept into his stomach.

Adler continued to study the drone. He didn't appear to push anything or even move his fingertips, but something abruptly sprang forth from the dented sphere.

Jasim leaped back. With his heart thudding in his chest, he stared at a needle on an articulating arm now thrusting from the surface of the drone. A patchwork of lines suggested other compartments, other things that could spring out. Like tools for cutting out cyborg implants? His mouth went dry. Blessings of the Suns Trinity, was he looking at the drone—or perhaps one of many drones—that had killed and cut up the other cyborgs?

"I presume the bikers were hired as a distraction," Leonidas said, then his tone turned bitter. "Four cyborgs' worth of implants would easily finance such things. And more."

"But how did he know we were here?" Jasim whispered.

"He might have only known one of us was here. The *Star Nomad* doesn't publicize its flight routes, but it does file them through the legal channels.

Or…" Leonidas eyed him. "Your skip tracer is getting paid by two different parties."

Jasim swallowed. "I don't think—"

"Brawling on the promenade is not permitted," one of the androids said, he and his partner stopping their bikes as they reached Adler and Jasim.

"Then it's good that you're here to put an end to it." Adler nodded at them, as if they were colleagues and on the same side. He said nothing about the dented drone in his hands, not even looking at it as he faced the androids.

Jasim said nothing, too busy pondering the myriad concerns whirling through his mind. *Could* McCall have betrayed them? She wasn't known for that. As far as Jasim had heard, bounty hunters and repo men weren't the only ones who hired her for her services. So did law enforcement agencies. She made good money—why would she need to betray her clients? If she *did* betray them, surely that would have gotten around.

Leonidas's suggestion that the *Star Nomad* had been tracked seemed more likely. If McCall hadn't been willing to work for Dufour, then he could have hired another skip tracer. If the man was systematically going down his list of Cyborg Corps men, as he seemed to be, then he must have been searching for Adler for a while. So maybe he'd moved quickly when he'd found him. Maybe he'd already had an operative on Primus 7 for some reason, so it had been easy for him to act, to have his operative program the drone and release it to target Adler. And the fact that Jasim had been along…maybe Dufour hadn't anticipated that. Maybe that was why he and Adler had succeeded in downing the bikers—and the drone—without being hurt. How much harder might this confrontation have been if Adler had been forced to fight everyone off alone? Would he have seen that drone zipping in from the side if Jasim hadn't been here to warn him?

"Damages have been done and humans injured," the android announced. "It is standard station procedure for all parties related to the skirmish to be detained."

"We were merely defending ourselves," Adler said.

Without waiting for further comments, and without letting go of the drone, he turned his back on the androids and walked over to get his armor case—it still rested next to the booth. Alas, the booth walls had numerous scorch marks and holes through them now, and the yarn display in the back had been destroyed, leaving charred bits of string dangling everywhere.

The android enforcers scrutinized Adler—he'd paused to pull out a comm unit—and one waved the spy box over. It flew around, collecting footage. Calculating damages? It paused in front of Jasim, and he bent over to adjust his boot, hoping it wasn't recording their faces, but that had probably already happened. The enforcers would get their identities, if they hadn't already, and likely send charges to his or Adler's ship. Or worse, Dufour might get ahold of the footage and know Jasim was helping Adler. Might he even suspect they were coming for him?

Jasim sighed and headed into the yarn booth.

"Ma'am?" He peered around the trunk, hoping she hadn't been hurt.

"Here, here," the woman said, skittering out from behind a stack of baskets. "Your yarn. No charge, take whatever you want." She pushed a bag at him while glancing toward the sausage kiosk and the crumpled android on the dented rooftop.

Jasim stared bleakly at her, not wanting the yarn for free—hells, he ought to pay for all the damages to her store, even if he hadn't started the fight. He also didn't want her to be afraid of him. *He* wasn't the thug here, not this time.

"Ready, Antar?" Adler asked from the front of the booth.

The two androids had their heads tilted, conferring silently, probably through the sys-net. Adler's nod toward them seemed to suggest that it would be a good idea to leave before they decided that anyone who had been involved in the fight should be arrested. Jasim agreed with the sentiment—and hoped the station's space traffic controller wouldn't keep the *Interrogator* from leaving its airlock—but he hated to leave the yarn seller in this state.

"Yes, sir. Be right there." Jasim faced the woman again. She'd scooted back, putting several feet between them. "Here," he said, pointing to his earstar. "I'm chipped and have Alliance tindarks in my account. Where's your charger?"

She lifted her hands. "No charge."

Jasim spotted the bank chip scanner on the floor, saw that she had started to list his purchases, and hit the total button, adding a big tip. He checked himself out, waving the scanner at his chip and hitting the process button.

"Thank you," he said, and jogged out, joining Adler.

Two more androids on bikes and in uniform sailed down the promenade toward the remains of the skirmish. One veered toward Jasim and Adler, but another android lifted his hand and pointed at Adler. "Not that one." He waved at the downed bikers. "Collect these for questioning and pressing charges."

"What about *that* one?" One of the new androids pointed at Jasim even as he strode away, hoping they wouldn't give chase.

The android who seemed to be in charge squinted, not at Jasim but at Adler. "No."

Glad for a lucky break, Jasim hurried into the lead so he could take Adler to his ship. He glanced at his old commander as they turned down the dock where the *Interrogator* waited. He had a feeling he wouldn't have walked away from that situation if he had been on his own. He remembered McCall's insinuation that Adler had new Alliance connections as well as old imperial ones. Could that have come into play out here? On a neutral station? Jasim decided that he'd done the right thing in bringing Adler in to help with this, even if walking beside his old commander made him feel uncomfortable, reminding him of his failings as a cyborg soldier. Besides, in addition to possibly having "connections," Adler could definitely still fight, especially for an "old man."

Adler squinted over at him, and Jasim realized he'd been smirking.

He wiped that expression clean, not wanting to explain his thoughts, and said, "Sorry about the delay, sir. It was important to get our bribe."

Adler peered at one of the bundles of yarn sticking out of the bag. "I see."

He would see even more in a few minutes, Jasim thought, turning toward Airlock 14.

"What are you planning to do with that?" Jasim asked, nodding toward the drone, then glancing back for the eighth or ninth time. He couldn't help but feel they might be followed, but once again, he did not see anyone. The throngs of people had returned to the promenade, and the androids and bikers were no longer visible.

"I commed someone from the *Nomad* to come pick it up before we leave."

"To be stored away in your collection of war trophies?"

Adler slid him a narrow-eyed look. "To be analyzed. She's my children's science tutor and has an ecumenical background. She may be able to identify the poison." He nodded toward the needle protruding from the drone. He was being careful to keep it facing away from his body.

Jasim did not know if identifying the poison would help them in any way. It killed people. Wasn't that enough to know? Still, he would happily hand the drone off to someone who might be able to glean information from its construction.

"Leonidas?" came a call from behind them, a slender bronze-skinned woman in her thirties waving and running to catch up to them. Clad in dirt-smudged overalls, she led a hoverboard stacked with recent purchases, sacks of "organic worm castings," whatever those were. They looked like bags of dirt.

Adler faced her. "Thank you for coming, Yumi. This is the item." He held up the drone.

She stopped several feet away, eyeing the needle for a moment before coming closer.

"I'd appreciate it if you examined it on the station somewhere instead of taking it aboard the ship. It could be dangerous."

"Less dangerous now, I imagine, than before someone put that giant dent in the side." The woman waved for him to lay the drone on her sacks of dirt. "I'll have Beck or Ostberg bring me some tools, and I'll take a look."

"Thank you. Send me whatever information you find, please."

"Will do." She waved again and led the hoverboard away.

Leonidas watched her go, his brow wrinkled with concern. He was probably worried that his family might be a target. Would he still be willing to leave them here?

"Do you want to wait to see what the results are?" Jasim asked. "And to make sure nothing else bad happens?"

"I trust Stanislav can protect the ship if there's any trouble," Leonidas murmured, the words seemingly more for himself than Jasim. But he did turn to Jasim and say, "I believe we should leave right away. Dufour will soon know that we're together, and he may guess that we're coming for him. Better not to give him extra time to plan."

"Yes, sir."

At Airlock 14, part of the sleek gray cylindrical shape of the *Interrogator* was visible through one of the expansive portholes. The ship appeared unmolested. Fortunately. Maddy could take care of herself, but Jasim did not want to bring any trouble to her hatch.

"This is the ship, sir," he said, waving Adler toward the airlock.

"You might as well call me Leonidas."

Jasim paused, his hand hanging in midair in front of the hatch controls.

"I don't command anything anymore," Adler added. The slightest bit wistfully?

Jasim remembered the gleam in his eyes during that skirmish. Did he miss the action of the Corps? The constant danger? The deaths of one's comrades? The killing of men and women who were only enemies because some high and mighty political schemer said so? Jasim could not imagine missing any of that. He would much rather have what Adler had now, a family and work that didn't devour his soul. He still wondered how the colonel had come by children and a wife, but he couldn't imagine broaching such a personal subject.

"Nothing at all?" Jasim asked, keeping his tone light. "Not even the children?"

"*Especially* not the children," Adler—Leonidas said dryly.

As they entered the ship, the thrum of the engines starting up reverberated through the deck. The hatch clanged shut behind them before Jasim closed it.

He hurried around the corner and into NavCom to make sure someone hadn't kidnapped Maddy. The yarn basket was still on the deck, and her familiar clipped-back gray hair was visible over the headrest.

"In a hurry, Maddy?" he asked.

She activated the thrusters, and they backed out of their docking spot. "After seeing you throw androids around out there? Figured we should go before trouble found us."

Jasim peered at the view screen. Had he and Leonidas been visible from here? No, the front of the ship was simply looking at the drab gray hull of the station.

"You're on the news," Maddy added, waving at jabbering heads on a holodisplay.

"That was quick," Leonidas murmured from behind Jasim.

Maddy squinted back at him. "That your armor smith?"

"Uhm, not exactly." Jasim wondered if she had poked her head into his cabin and seen that he hadn't taken his armor case with him when he left.

"Leaving is a good idea," Leonidas said, looking at Jasim instead of Maddy, as if he believed him to be in charge.

And why wouldn't he? The great Colonel Adler wouldn't expect one of his former elite cyborg soldiers to be taking orders from a seventy-year-old woman wearing a bird sweater.

"I don't know who you are," Maddy told Leonidas, looking fearlessly at him, "but I wasn't planning to take on passengers when I stopped here. Just some fresh and sparkly cyborg armor." She raised her eyebrows at Jasim.

He flushed, aware of Leonidas looking at him. *Yes, sir, I lied to my pilot, just as I did to Mental Health Services all those years ago, trying to escape the military…*

And here he thought he had grown up.

"I haven't told her about the murderer yet," he told Leonidas. "It's not her problem. And this isn't technically my ship."

"Technically?" Maddy asked. "It's not even untechnically your ship. You're lucky I let you out of your cabin to breathe my son-in-law's expensive air."

"You'd have trouble knitting me things if you didn't let me out occasionally," Jasim mumbled, looking at Leonidas's collarbone instead of into his eyes, afraid he'd see disgust there. Yes, he had a lowly job, and yes, he took orders from Granny Madeline.

Leonidas did not say anything.

Maddy didn't have any trouble finding words. "Earl wants us to head to Sepiron Station next." If she was curious about his comment about a murderer, she did not show it. "A couple of ships got left there after their owners supposedly fled from debt collectors. But one of those debt collectors turned up dead, so Earl thinks the owners or maybe some squatters are there, keeping the ships from getting picked up. He said to take you to handle it. *Just* you." She waved at Leonidas, perhaps indicating he could see himself out, no matter that they weren't attached to the station anymore.

Jasim looked at Leonidas, who merely looked down at the yarn bag. Yes, the yarn. Jasim had known Maddy would have a fit, and he'd planned for it. He'd just hoped he wouldn't have to wheedle in front of his old C.O.

"Actually," Jasim said, stepping over the knitting basket so he could sit in the co-pilot's seat facing Maddy. He had to lift needles and the three-quarters-finished scarf out of it so he didn't prong himself in the butt. "My…friend here and I have a problem and need to swing by Dustor for a brief stop."

Maddy scowled at him as she flipped switches. "You don't *swing by* Dustor. It's out in the armpit of the system. It would take almost two weeks of flying to get there, stay long enough to spit in the sand, and then fly to Sepiron Station. Instead of three days. My son-in-law doesn't pay us to make *brief stops*. This isn't a sightseeing ship. Nor did you tell me that there would be an extra passenger." She glowered at Leonidas again. "A *huge* extra passenger. It's bad enough feeding you. How much does he eat? I didn't order that many rat packs."

"I can pilot the ship if necessary," Leonidas said.

"What is *that* supposed to mean?" Maddy asked, her glower turning into a deep scowl.

Jasim caught the gist right away, that Leonidas was offering to fly if they locked Maddy in her cabin for the duration of the trip. That would only get Jasim in more trouble. A *lot* more trouble. One did not lock up The Pulverizer's mother-in-law.

"Maddy, won't you consider diverting to Dustor?" he said, smiling and holding open the bag. "There's someone who's been murdering cyborgs, and I may be next on the list. I recruited help here, as you can see, and I'm sure it won't take long. Once we're on Dustor. Look, I brought you something that could keep you occupied for those extra days in space."

"You think you can *bribe* me?" She might have sounded indignant if she hadn't been leaning over and peering into the bag.

Jasim decided not to be offended that she seemed far more interested in the bribe than in the fact that a murderer was after him.

"I bet there's something we could repossess on Dustor while we're there," Jasim added.

"I doubt it. Nobody takes nice things to Dustor. Nobody takes *anything* to Dustor if they can help it, including themselves. Earl will never approve of that long a detour. Huh, is that Teravian wool? Where did you find this? Just out on the promenade? I had no idea they had such exotic imports. I should have gone shopping while you were gone."

"Maybe The Pulverizer wouldn't have to know about Dustor," Jasim suggested. "Perhaps he could believe we were delayed here because we had to deal with some mechanical problems."

Maddy frowned at him. "You want me to lie to my son-in-law?"

"Perhaps just an omission of certain information."

"He looks at the odometers on the ships when they're turned in. Even if I were the dishonest sort, which I'm not, he'd know we logged some extra miles." She poked into the bag, examining the various offerings. "Besides, it's not as if I *need* to lie to him. If I want to go somewhere else, I go. Who do you think gave him the money to start up his little business? Is that Rainbow Sheen there on the bottom?"

Leonidas leaned against the hatchway and stuck a hand in his pocket. He wore a contemplative expression, as if he was still considering locking her up for the trip. Or maybe he was wondering if his former corporal would grow some balls and stand up to this grandmother instead of trying to bribe her.

"I believe you," Jasim told Maddy, figuring he had better wrap this up quickly, before Leonidas lost patience and arranged for his own transportation. If Jasim walked out on Maddy, he'd be walking out on his hopes of continued employment, too, and he needed his job. At least for now. "You're a strong, independent woman, Maddy. You go where you want to go."

"Yes, I do." She leaned back, tapping the controls. "And if you think I want to go to Dustor, you're delusional."

"Please, Maddy?" Jasim set the bag of yarn down on top of her knitting basket. "I'd consider it a personal favor. And so would Leonidas. That's why we brought a gift."

She looked back at Leonidas, and his eyebrows drifted upward again as she scrutinized him more thoroughly than she had before. Almost…lasciviously, Jasim thought, as her gaze lingered in certain key areas. By the suns, what kind of *gift* did she think Jasim had meant?

"He's wearing a wedding ring," Maddy said. "And he looks like a soldier."

"Aren't those things all right?"

"I'd much rather have a gift from one of the male prostitutes you got me thinking about."

"I—er." What was he supposed to say to that?

"It's been three years since my husband died, you know. A woman gets lonely."

Jasim thought Leonidas would be scandalized—or at least horrified.

All Leonidas said was, "We ought to be able to find prostitutes on Dustor."

"I want a handsome, young man," Maddy said. "A handsome, young *gentleman*. I'm not into the rough stuff anymore."

"We agree to your terms," Leonidas said.

Jasim rubbed a hand down his face.

"Setting in a course for Dustor," Maddy said.

"What just happened?" Jasim asked Leonidas.

"Your first bribe was insufficient," Leonidas informed him. "You're going to need to find her someone to knit with while we're busy."

"I don't know how to find prostitutes. I'm—" He glanced at Maddy and stopped. As far as he knew, the fact that imperial cyborgs were essentially neutered as part of their surgery wasn't widely known, and he didn't care to talk about it with outsiders, regardless. "I'm not familiar with Dustor's services and amenities," he finished, his cheeks reddening.

"Perhaps your skip tracer friend can help," Leonidas suggested. His eyes had that gleam in them again. Was he *amused* by this?

Jasim hadn't even thought his commander could *be* amused. Certainly nobody had spoken of his sense of humor when he'd been in charge of the Corps.

"I wonder what I'd have to get the dog for that information," Jasim muttered, rubbing his face again.

CHAPTER SEVEN

The smell of smoke clung to Leonidas's armor and the insides of his nostrils. Odd that it lingered here on the admiral's ship. Odd, too, that he was noticing it now, with intense pain radiating out from his chest, throbbing with each step, or maybe with each beat of his heart. He was lucky the lance had missed his heart. From the way he was coughing up blood, he was fairly certain his left lung hadn't been so lucky. Not surprising when the broken end of the weapon was still sticking out of his chest, still crackling faintly with the energy that had given it the power to break through his nearly indestructible armor.

An alarm klaxon wailed in the distance, and Leonidas halted in the middle of the corridor. Had the rebels returned with more ships? Was the Stellar Dart in danger? The civilians and the wounded had been moved to this ship because it was undamaged and supposedly fast enough to evade the rebel terrorists. But if it was threatened, he couldn't continue to sickbay. He had to be ready to go back into battle.

"Keep moving, Major," the doctor behind him said.

Leonidas started to look over his shoulder, but that hurt too much. He clenched his fist, annoyed with the injury.

"Keep moving, or I'll go find that hover gurney you refused to ride on earlier."

Though the alarms concerned him, Leonidas continued down the corridor. Logically, he knew he had to have the lance removed, his lung repaired, and the rest of the wound sealed before he could be effective in combat again.

"I don't think captains are supposed to give majors orders," he grumbled as he walked, refusing to put his hand on the bulkhead for support, though his legs were numb, and he wasn't sure enough oxygen was getting to them. It was probably all leaking out of his chest with his blood.

"I'm a doctor and the head of sickbay, and you're injured. I definitely get to give you orders. Anyone in my sickbay does, even the privates. Turn left at the intersection."

"I don't need directions," he said, annoyed when the words turned into coughs. Even if he hadn't been aboard the Dart *before, Leonidas knew the layouts of all the imperial ships in the fleet.*

"I see you're going to be a delightful patient," the doctor said, jogging around Leonidas to lead the way into sickbay. "Someone get me a crowbar so we can get this cyborg out of his turtle shell," he hollered.

This cyborg. Not this soldier. Or this man.

Leonidas curled his lip. "I'll get my armor off on my own," he said, tossing his helmet onto the nearest flat surface.

More gingerly, he removed his big assault rifle, which hung on a strap across his torso. Lifting his arm to pull it over his head tripled his pain and threatened to drop him to his knees. But he saw a couple of familiar faces in the row of beds lining the wall. Two of his own men were among the injured, Zimmer and Alvarado. They lay propped up in their beds, both staring at him. Zimmer's shirt was off, revealing bandages wrapping his torso and burns up and down his arms. Some healing gel had already been slathered along them. Alvarado—hells, he'd lost his leg. A medical device was fastened to the stump, no doubt doing its best to mend and prepare him for a prosthetic, but he'd never be able to return to the unit.

"The major's here," Alvarado said, grinning despite his grievous injury. He even reached over to bump fists with Zimmer. "Maybe now we can get some beer."

"I don't know, Sergeant. He's got a…Sir, is that an imploder *lance through your chest?" Zimmer asked, leaning his head to see around Leonidas's back as he set down his rifle. "Blessed Suns Trinity, it went all the way through. Aren't those supposed to be for taking down ships?"*

"Well, the major's almost as big as a ship."

Leonidas only shook his head, not particularly wanting to explain how he'd been foolish enough to get hit. Oh, the part where he'd been pushing the admiral out of the way so he wouldn't be hit by those damn assassins wasn't embarrassing, just the part where he'd tripped over a body and been too slow to keep himself from being struck. By the suns, he was getting old.

"There is a resemblance," Zimmer said. "I can see how the enemy would have been confused."

"You two are awfully perky for injured men," Leonidas growled, which turned into coughing up blood. The doctor frowned over at him—he'd paused to grab a couple of nurses to help with the armor removal, but he hurried over now and guided Leonidas to a bed next to Alvarado.

"Barely injured," Zimmer said. *"Look, my skin is already growing back."*

"Too bad that goo won't do anything for your brain cells," Alvarado said.

"I didn't get hit in the head."

"And yet…damage."

Zimmer glared at him. *"Don't think I won't kick your ass just because there's only one leg attached to it."*

The doctor and nurses surrounded Leonidas's bed, and he did not see the return glare, if there was one. More likely, Alvarado would stick his tongue out.

The doctor pressed an auto-injector to Leonidas's neck, some drug deploying with a soft, cold hiss.

"You knocking me out?" Leonidas asked, feeling numbness creep through his body immediately.

"To operate on you, yes."

"I didn't ask for that."

"And yet, everyone here would prefer you unconscious. Your sergeant there accidentally knocked Corporal Rigger across sickbay when he touched a sensitive spot."

"He didn't touch it," Alvarado said. *"He stabbed it with a tool sharper and pokier than the doc's prick."*

The doctor glared over at him and shook his head. *"You people are as dangerous to your own side as the enemy."*

"I should be awake in case the situation escalates again," Leonidas said, ignoring the *"you people"* comment, though it irked him. It wasn't as if they weren't all human here.

"The space station was blown to a zillion pieces," the doctor said. *"What's left to escalate?"*

"We better be going after those damn anarchists," Leonidas growled. *"Targeting civilian installations. If we hadn't been heading this way for an inspection…"*

"You wouldn't have a spear sticking out of your chest."

"They would have gotten away with it," Leonidas said. Some of them had, but many more hadn't. Even though he'd only had a small squad of men here, he and the fleet soldiers aboard the ship had saved a lot of lives on the station—and utterly destroyed three of the four rebel ships docked there. If only that fourth one hadn't gotten away…if

only Leonidas hadn't had to divide his men to make sure the admiral, who'd insisted on boarding the station, was protected…

"We'll get 'em back, sir," Alvarado said, his voice sounding farther away than the next bed now that the drug was taking hold. "You wait and see. We'll squash 'em like roaches under our boots. Alliance, they call themselves. They're anarchists and terrorists. It won't take long to flush 'em out of hiding and get rid of 'em all."

Leonidas, who had heard the reports from Intel, knew it wouldn't be as easy as that, but all he said was, "You're a good man, Alvarado."

"Nah, I'm just trying to cheer everybody up, especially the doctor there, in the hope that beer will be forthcoming."

Leonidas had a notion of ordering someone to find his man a beer, but the drug took over first, and he dropped into unconsciousness.

Leonidas shook away his memories and refocused on the holodisplay floating over his netdisc. He pushed his hand through his hair, surprised how well he remembered that day. They hadn't known it at the time, but it had been the opening salvo of the war. Alvarado had been in therapy for months, learning to use his new leg, and Leonidas had been wrong. He *had* been sent back to the unit. It had been clear by then that the empire needed all of its cyborgs for the war, even the less than optimal ones. When he'd been in his combat armor, Alvarado hadn't been noticeably weaker than anyone, and he'd never complained, not within Leonidas's hearing. And if he'd done it anywhere else, Leonidas hadn't heard about it. Not like some of the other men, the ones who'd complained about splinters. And mental health issues.

He looked toward the closed hatch of the small cabin he had been given. Jasim's cabin was across the corridor.

He sighed and forced uncharitable thoughts aside. He'd long ago learned that who lived and died had nothing to do with fairness or who was the better person, and that wishing it could be otherwise was an exercise in futility. Besides, Leonidas was well aware that he himself hadn't been the best among his men, promotions notwithstanding. Nor was he without flaws. If logic and merit decided the fates of men, he never would have made it out of the war.

And judging Jasim today based on the youth Leonidas remembered wasn't fair. He hadn't shied away during that skirmish on the promenade.

Leonidas didn't think he'd shied away from battle years earlier, either—at least, nothing like that had made it into the reports that came to his desk—which was surprising given how badly he'd wanted to get out of the military.

Leonidas swiped a finger through the holodisplay, going back to the work he'd been doing before the memories made him pause. He had pulled up the names and last known addresses for as many of the men who had been in the Cyborg Corps during the war as he could remember. The roster wasn't public information—he'd already checked—and the secure sys-net site where he'd once logged in to access imperial military data had been down for years. He was doing his best, however, so he could send warning messages to everyone he could contact. Unfortunately, fewer than half the men were easily found. Some had changed names, some were living off the grid, and some had simply disappeared.

He thought of Malik, the sergeant who had turned pirate and slaver, and who was now dead. He also remembered Sergeant Lancer, who had died in Leonidas's arms on Starfall Station. How many of his people, people who had been designed to be difficult to kill and who had survived years of battle, had died for no good reason after the empire fell? After the purpose for which they'd been created no longer existed?

He sighed again, feeling lucky that he'd found another purpose. Even if he sometimes grew antsy traveling on the freighter, leading a largely sedate life as a family man, Alisa and the kids made him feel needed. Important. Still, he admitted that the peace and quiet of this ship felt extremely restful after having the twins around all the time. And Jelena wasn't exactly a noiseless mouse either. Just last week, she'd talked Ostberg into helping her build a zip line in the cargo hold—without asking for permission. He felt a little ashamed for relishing the peace and the solitude—and enjoying the anticipation he felt for what could be a battle waiting for him.

"Hm," Leonidas murmured to himself, tapping a name on the display. "Here's someone living on Dustor."

Rick Banding. He had started a pawnshop in Port Thorn a year earlier.

Leonidas fired off a warning and asked Banding—Corporal Banding, he recalled—to comm him back. If the killer continued down the alphabetical list, Banding could be one of the next targets. That might motivate him to close down his shop for a few days and help with the investigation. Leonidas suspected he and Jasim could handle the murderer by themselves, assuming they could find him, but Banding might be less likely to be taken out if he was with them. Whoever was doing this had to be crafty. As Alisa had said, cyborgs weren't easy to kill.

A knock sounded at the hatch.

"Yes?" Leonidas asked, shifting awkwardly to stand up without hitting his head on the top bunk. His tiny cabin did not have any furniture except for the two built-in beds and a couple of storage cabinets—and his armor case, which rested on the floor by the head of the lower bunk.

"Was that an invitation to come in, sir?" Jasim asked from the corridor.

"Leonidas," he corrected, opening the hatch.

Jasim stood there, his too-long hair pulled back into a sloppy bun. Leonidas managed to keep from curling his lip at the un-soldierly style.

"I know, sir," he said, his gaze shifting uneasily.

Maybe he felt Leonidas's disapproval. Leonidas tried to smooth his face. It was a silly thing to even think about.

"But it's an old habit," Jasim continued. "We're a few hours out from Dustor."

Leonidas nodded. Good, it wouldn't take his message to Banding long to reach the planet, then.

"Have you gotten news back on the drone?" Jasim asked.

"Yes, Yumi sent me a complete report yesterday. She agreed that the contents of the injector were a deadly poison, but she cross-checked numerous sources and didn't find anything out there like it, at least not in the public domain. She hypothesizes that the poison was custom-made to work on large people with fast metabolisms who process drugs quickly."

"Such as cyborgs."

"Such as cyborgs," Leonidas agreed. "She opened up the drone casing with our engineer's help and found extendable cutting tools, as well as an internal storage area."

"Cutting tools capable of removing a cyborg's implants, I assume."

Leonidas nodded. "But there wasn't any identification on the drone, not even a manufacturer's mark. It seems it was also a custom piece."

"Our man has been planning this for a while. He must have more than one of those drones too. There were attacks on different planets at nearly the same time."

"It seems likely, yes."

Jasim didn't say anything else, but he also didn't back away. Did he want something more?

Leonidas lifted his eyebrows.

"Ah, I was wondering if you wanted to spar or do drills together, sir. There's some open space near the engine room in the back." Jasim waved down the ship's single corridor.

Yes, Leonidas had found the spot a couple of days ago. He'd been doing exercises back there on his own, being a little disappointed that Jasim didn't have any gym equipment set up. But it wasn't, he reminded himself, Jasim's ship. Maybe his employer would object to cyborg comforts.

"You don't think those bikers we sparred with were sufficient to keep us in shape?" Leonidas asked, but he did flex his shoulders, interested in the idea. He wouldn't mind pitting himself against another person, someone with the strength and agility to challenge him. He'd brought his hover pads along, but he had been busy researching the whereabouts of his former battalion for most of the trip.

"I don't know what we'll face," Jasim said, "and I haven't had anyone to drill with in a while. I've been in fights enough, I suppose, but that's not quite the same. And I wasn't sure if you'd…" Jasim's gaze shifted to the top of Leonidas's head—to his hair. "You handled yourself well on Primus 7, of course, but it's been a while since the war, and I wasn't sure if you have anyone on your ship you can drill with either."

Leonidas let his eyelids droop. "Are you suggesting I might be old and out of shape?"

It hadn't occurred to him that Jasim might be judging him, even as he was judging Jasim. Even though Leonidas knew he was getting older, and that younger cyborgs had the advantage of more recent—and more technologically advanced—implants, as well as the speed of youth, he prided himself on staying fit.

"I just—no, sir. What I meant to say was that I would be honored if you sparred with me and instructed me with the wisdom of your years."

Leonidas snorted. "You're lousy at sucking up. It was better when you were implying I was old and out of shape. At least it was honest."

"Sorry, sir."

Jasim genuinely seemed to be—at the least he was being contrite around his former commander. Leonidas hadn't yet seen much evidence of the prankster who had stolen other men's undergarments in the middle of the night for fun. He supposed everybody grew up eventually.

"I'll get my hover pads and meet you back there," Leonidas said, nodding toward the rear of the vessel.

"Good." Jasim lifted his hand, as if to salute, but stopped in the middle and turned it into a wave. Looking flustered, he jogged out of sight.

Leonidas opened his armor case for the first time since leaving the *Nomad*. A delightful scent met his nose, one far different from the usual odor of sanitizer. He pulled out a container of brownies and a few folded pieces of paper, some with writing on them, others with colored pictures on them. He swallowed a lump that formed in his throat. Notes from Alisa and the kids.

Since Jasim was waiting, he put them aside to read later. He felt touched that they had thought to prepare them—he now wished he'd left something behind for them—but he also felt guilty all over again for enjoying this break.

Jasim was in the compact space in the rear of the ship, the last open space before the engine room. Luggage, supplies, and crates of non-perishable food lined the walls. After the spaciousness of the *Nomad's* cargo hold, it was a cramped place to spar, or do anything, but Jasim had a battered set of his own hover pads out, punches connecting with the floating targets. They zipped and swooped about him to make it challenging.

When he saw Leonidas, Jasim powered them down and tossed them into a corner. "Did you bring your wisdom, sir?" he asked, waving his fingers in invitation.

"We'll see." Leonidas placed his own hover pads on a crate.

They came together in silent agreement, starting with a series of jabs, punches, and blocks that were familiar drills for both of them. Leonidas hadn't typically sparred with, or even instructed, the younger soldiers once he'd been promoted above lieutenant, but he had often worked out with other officers, and they had done similar drills. Performing them again now reminded him of those days, and he fell into the patterns easily. Neither he nor Jasim tried hard to hit each other during this warm-up. Unfortunately, the exercises also reminded Leonidas that most of those officers he had once trained with were now dead. It was uncomfortable to get to a point in one's life when all of one's peers were dead. Even though he barely knew Jasim, and he hadn't been the shining star of the Corps, it felt surprisingly good to be around someone from the old unit again, someone with all the same problems that he dealt with, someone who understood what it was like to be a cyborg. To be both more and less than human, at least to the rest of the universe. Leonidas had never considered himself anything but a man.

"Can I ask you something, sir?" Jasim asked after they had worked up a sweat.

"Yes." Leonidas stepped back and lowered his hands.

It wouldn't surprise him if more than a need for exercise had prompted Jasim to knock on his hatch. If nothing else, he had been expecting a question about how he had come to be married with children. He had already directed a few curious cyborgs he'd encountered to Dr. Tiang, the imperial-turned-Alliance brain surgeon who had operated on him. He had almost died during the operation, though, thanks to the traps the empire had planted in his brain to keep outsiders from tampering, so it wasn't something to be undertaken lightly.

"Your captain—your wife…" Jasim turned away and walked toward a towel he'd brought out with him. "Did you get a job working for her before you became…friends?" He grimaced, looking as uncomfortable as he sounded.

Leonidas wasn't sure what to make of the question. It wasn't the one he had expected.

"Technically, yes. We were flying in some dangerous areas right after the war. A cyborg security officer is a boon on any team, if a slight demotion for a former imperial officer." Slight was an understatement, but by the time he'd accepted Alisa's offer, the *Star Nomad* had been on the hunt for an ancient Starseer artifact and the missing Prince Thorian, both objectives that he had believed necessary to pursue. The prince because Leonidas had given his word to the emperor that he would make sure his son was kept safe, and the artifact because he hadn't wanted it to fall into Alliance hands. The Alliance had enough power these days.

"Security officer." Jasim grimaced again. "Is that what you were? I thought...never mind."

"Security, yes." Leonidas frowned. Surely, Jasim wasn't judging him for that. It wasn't as if repossessing people's valuables was some far nobler and loftier employment.

"Was there ever any question of...was the captain nervous about you being around her daughter?"

Leonidas's frown deepened. What *was* he implying? "No."

"She trusted you not to hurt anyone or be...inappropriate because you were a soldier? A cyborg soldier? Someone who had..." He lowered his towel and studied the palms of his hands. "Someone who had killed."

Leonidas forced the frown off his face, realizing this wasn't about him. Jasim probably wasn't trying to insult him. He was curious about something, but Leonidas didn't quite know what.

"She knew me well by the time her daughter came aboard," Leonidas said.

"Ah. What would you do if people wouldn't give you a chance?" Jasim lowered his hands. "Wouldn't take the time to get to know you well?"

Leonidas opened his mouth, but their pilot walked in then, carrying two long knitting needles and what looked like most of a scarf dangling from them, the end draped over her shoulder.

"We're not far from Dustor," she said. "Who's paying the docking fee for this excursion?"

"I am," Jasim said before Leonidas could offer.

He hustled past the woman—Maddy, Leonidas recalled—and up the corridor. Had he not truly wanted an answer to his question? Or maybe he'd known there wasn't a good answer. Plenty of people had judged Leonidas prematurely by his reputation or simply by the way he looked. Everyone got that though. Not just cyborgs. And of all the people in the system, surely cyborgs could take care of themselves if they were mistreated by someone. Still, he admitted that enhanced body parts didn't do anything to take away the sting of perceived slights.

"You a cyborg too?" Maddy, still in the compartment, asked, looking him up and down.

"Yes." Leonidas did not know what to make of the woman, but would attempt to keep from offending her, since she seemed to be a direct conduit to Jasim's employer.

"You ever do repo work? My son-in-law's always looking to hire good men. He might want you to dye that hair to look younger and more intimidating, but you've probably considered that anyway."

Leonidas lifted his eyebrows. "Have you considered dyeing yours?"

"Nah, not recently. I did follicle mods back when I first started graying, but they made my scalp itch. Besides—" she waved a knitting needle at her head, "—sometimes it pays to have people underestimate you."

"Perhaps I subscribe to the same school of thought."

She prodded one of his biceps with her needle. "I'm thinking not."

Leonidas was about to point out that she would be needed at the helm soon if they were approaching Dustor, but she spoke again.

"Do you want a hat?"

"What?"

"I'm almost done with Jasim's scarf, and I have all that new yarn." Maddy looked expectantly at him.

A few days ago, she hadn't wanted him on her ship, and he hadn't gone out of his way to speak to her since then, preferring to keep to his cabin and do his research. Maybe she had decided he was worth talking to—or knitting for—because she wanted to recruit him for the family business. Or maybe it was because he'd helped Jasim come up with a suitable bribe for her. Leonidas had no idea how that would play out, but he was certain Alisa would find it amusing if he told her about it.

"I make hats of all kinds." Maddy shrugged. "You can come up and pick your color. Or colors. And let me measure your head. It's a big one, isn't it?"

"It's normal."

"You cyborgs are anything but normal." Maddy waved her needle again and headed for the corridor. "Let me know if you want a job in our outfit. And don't forget to bring your head by for measuring. Preferably when it's not sweaty." She kept talking even as she walked out of sight.

"Do you like tassels? A few tassels might soften that hard jaw of yours. You wouldn't want to repo wearing them, but you're married, right? I'm sure your lady will enjoy the style. A few tassels can make a man look playful and friendly."

Leonidas scratched his head. Why were pilots always odd?

CHAPTER EIGHT

Walking out into the hot, dry air of Dustor was like stepping into a sauna. Jasim wore his combat armor, but he hadn't yet donned the helmet, so he felt the heat. The gazes of hard-eyed, rough people raked over him, men and women walking through the docking area. Maybe he *should* put on his helmet. None of those people looked like they had a love for cyborgs. What was new?

Jasim checked the blazer rifle he wore across his armored torso in addition to the smaller weapons integrated into the arm pieces of his suit. In a utility belt, he carried a knife and a few tools for thwarting locks and energy windows.

Leonidas stepped through the hatch after him, ducking his head to do so. He, too, wore his armor. Jasim did not comment on the childish stickers adorning it, one on his calf, one on his back, and one on his shoulder.

From what Jasim had seen of the kids, he could easily imagine them enjoying dressing Dad up. For some reason, the thought made him feel wistful. He'd never considered the idea of children of his own, figuring teaching would be the closest he could get, but maybe he should ask Leonidas for the name of that doctor he mentioned. He wished he hadn't chickened out halfway through asking his other questions. He'd been hoping that Leonidas had found a way around his reputation as a super soldier and a killer to find a job that didn't involve killing or roughing people up, but if he'd originally been hired as a security officer, then he hadn't. People had seen him the same way they saw Jasim. Even the woman who had become his wife had in the beginning, it seemed. Still, Leonidas appeared to be well connected, a rare thing for a cyborg in the aftermath of the empire's fall. Jasim wouldn't mind asking him for help or maybe a reference. But that would be presumptuous. Jasim didn't think Leonidas liked him or respected him. Why would he want to vouch for Jasim in any way? He was here to help out the old unit, not Jasim. Earning his respect seemed an insurmountable obstacle.

"I'm ready," Leonidas said, perhaps wondering why Jasim was standing in the walkway without moving.

"Me too." Jasim headed away from the ship.

Their plan was to visit their old colleague Corporal Banding before heading to the address McCall had given them, but that colleague hadn't answered Leonidas's message, so they didn't know what they would find. His pawnshop was reputedly still open, so he hadn't locked up and gone off on a trip or vacation. Jasim hoped they weren't heading into the city to find another body. The killer wouldn't skip to B-surnames before he'd finished the A's, would he?

"I see Dustor is as hospitable as ever," Leonidas said, his gaze scanning the docks and the buildings beyond, many of the old walls adorned with graffiti. People in ragged clothing sat or lay in out-of-the-way nooks along the cracked sidewalks. A few made superstitious signs when Leonidas and Jasim walked by in their armor.

"Not much in the system is hospitable to cyborgs anymore." Jasim eyed Leonidas. "Do you mind if I ask how you came to have Alliance contacts?" Jasim hoped he wasn't prying, but if his contacts might be useful in their investigation, it was worth asking about. "People don't seem that eager to bother you when they figure out who you are."

"Except for the cyborg killer? He and his drones don't seem to mind bothering me." Leonidas's lips thinned. "He better not have bothered my family."

Jasim agreed with the sentiment. He had no family of his own left, but he could see why Leonidas would value what he had.

"I meant other people," Jasim said. "Like security androids on space stations."

"Our ship's chef catered Senator Hawk's wedding a few years ago."

"That old freighter has a chef?" Jasim asked, almost as surprised by that as by the loose implication that Leonidas might have been at that Alliance senator's wedding. Of all the people who had reasons to hate cyborgs, former Alliance military officers were at the top of the list, and Jasim recalled that Senator Hawk had been *Admiral* Hawk, one of their star pilots, before retiring into politics.

"He started out as a security officer too," Leonidas said, his tone dry. It wasn't all that inviting so Jasim didn't ask more. Knowing a senator on the other side of the system probably wouldn't be of much use here on Dustor.

"You know which way to go, sir?" Jasim asked. They had reached the end of the docks, and an intersection offered several possible routes into the city.

"The pawnshop is this way." Leonidas pointed in one direction, but looked back toward the docks before heading that way. "Will your pilot be all right without a guard?"

"She'll keep the hatch shut. I doubt anyone will harass her." Jasim waved at the side of the ship where The Pulverizer's name and double-axes logo stretched along the hull. "He's fairly well-known on planets like this. Besides, she has numerous weapons if someone does try to get in."

"Such as knitting needles?"

"A destroyer, too, and there's a weapons locker with rifles in it. She knows how to use them."

"She offered to knit me a hat," Leonidas said as they headed into the city.

The smells of body odor, grease, and urine wafting out of alleys made Jasim think that he should don his helmet, if only to take advantage of the filtration system.

"She's knitted countless hats, sweaters, and socks for her dozen-odd grandchildren," he said. "I read between the lines that she may have been forbidden to send more. I know The Pulverizer has rejected offers for her to outfit his office staff. I heard that exchange. So she knits things for almost everyone she comes across now."

"Does she offer everyone tassels?"

"Uh, I don't think so. You must be special, sir." Jasim considered his somewhat craggy features and strong, hard jaw. "Or maybe you just have a tassel face."

"Undoubtedly."

They walked in silence, waving away robocabs that slowed down, offering to take them wherever they wished for an exorbitant price. The graffiti and blazer scorch marks on the sides of the vehicles did not inspire notions of safety and reliability. Human hustlers replaced robot ones when Jasim and Leonidas turned down an alley, the cinderblock walls windowless, and only intermittent doors with signs hanging on them suggesting that goods and services could be purchased within. Security guards stood next to a few of the doors.

Leonidas pointed to the end of the alley at a sign for the Banding Pawn Mecca.

Jasim remembered the man they were looking for, Corporal Banding. They had been about the same age, same time in service, and they'd done a few assignments together. Banding had been easygoing and hadn't said anything the time he had been on C.Q. and caught Jasim smearing the inside of Sergeant Gonzales's shirt with depilation cream. Of course, Sergeant Gonzales had definitely deserved it. Everyone had laughed the next day, when he was complaining about his bald chest. Jasim didn't know how successful this pawnshop was, but he felt encouraged that one of their kind had managed to start a business.

There weren't any guards standing outside of the thick sandstone door. Jasim waved his hand at a sensor, but it did not open. He tried a latch, and it did not budge.

Leonidas tapped a button on a panel to the side of the door.

"Store is not open outside of posted hours," a mechanical voice said.

"It's the middle of the day," Jasim said, confirming that they were within the hours when it should be open.

Leonidas knocked, insomuch as one could on a stone door. It was more of a thumping.

"I'm starting to think we're not going to find anything good here," Jasim asked.

"Maybe he broke for lunch," Leonidas said, but his face was grim.

"Should we force our way in?" Jasim looked up and down the alley, eyeing the handful of security guards near the other shops. There was enough foot traffic that they might not notice if he and Leonidas forced their way in quietly. Or they might not *care* if they forced their way in. This was Dustor, after all.

Leonidas leaned his armored shoulder against the door. Instead of making a show of ramming it, he simply crouched and pushed. The locking mechanism snapped, and he shoved the door open.

Lights came on inside, and a couple of robots rolled out from behind display cases and racks. Jasim's first thought was that they were there for security purposes, but they asked in unison, "How may we help you?"

"We're looking for the owner," Leonidas said. "Rick Banding."

"We have blazer rifles, pistols, grenade launchers, all-terrain assault vehicles, fire sprayers, and more," one robot said. "Would you like to peruse our brochure?"

A holodisplay popped into the air between the robot and Leonidas, showing images and specifications for many of the items it had listed.

"Not exactly a gold and diamonds kind of place, is it?" Jasim asked, looking around at racks of weapons. He spotted a tank in a rear corner and wondered how Banding had gotten it in here. There weren't any larger doors anywhere, just another person-sized one in the back. "Must be what the local clientele wants. Apparently, nobody on Dustor longs to buy gifts for a wife or girlfriend. Unless the wife or girlfriend has a fondness for assault rifles."

"We'll look around," Leonidas told the robot, shooing it aside.

The no-nonsense colonel, as Jasim remembered him.

He followed as Leonidas strode past display stands and under a large holovid that came on near the ceiling, showing people in desert camouflage out in the Dustor Dune Sea, sniping at the giant worms that lived out there, munching on men who wandered into their domain.

Leonidas passed aisles capped with stacks of dehydrated goods and cases of grenades and knocked on the back door. Once again, there was no answer, and it was locked. Jasim joined him as he broke the lock with a snap and pushed it open.

"Do you think it's within your right as a man's former commanding officer to break his doors?" Jasim asked.

Leonidas gave him a flat look, and Jasim shut his mouth. This wasn't the time for jokes. He reminded himself that he'd hoped to win the colonel's respect, not irk him.

They passed into a short windowless hall. The lights did not come on this time, nor did any robots roll out to greet them. They checked three doors, which led to an office, a small kitchen, and a bathroom. A netdisc lay atop a desk in the office, a signal flashing: a message waiting. Leonidas's warning that trouble was brewing and he was coming? Had it arrived too late?

Jasim started to move on to the last room, an open door at the end of the hall, and memories of discovering Adams's body came to mind. This was too damn similar. Except that in the case of Banding, Jasim actually liked the man. Nobody would miss Adams, but Banding had been a decent fellow.

He paused when he realized Leonidas had stopped at the bathroom. He gazed upward toward something inside.

"What is it, sir?" Jasim asked, coming back to join him—happy to put off looking in what was likely the bedroom.

Leonidas pointed at a high window on the far wall of the bathroom. After a second of study, Jasim realized it wasn't a window at all, at least not an official one. Above the sanibox, a circle had been cut in the cinderblock, and a beam of sunlight slanted in. A hint of the stink from the streets outside filtered in too. The longer Jasim looked at it, the less likely he deemed it that Banding had installed the unorthodox window. Scorch marks blackened the wall around the opening, and a few chips had fallen away from the stone.

"That hole looks big enough for one of those drones," Leonidas said.

"Yes, sir," Jasim said grimly. "Looks like it was done recently. Are we too late?"

"We'll find out." Leonidas headed down the hall toward the last door.

By now, Jasim expected to find Banding on the floor or dead in his bed with a tiny pinprick hole in his throat and all his implants cut out. He took a breath, steeling himself before he walked through the doorway. The bed was rumpled, with a blanket on the floor, but there was nobody in the room.

"Huh," Jasim uttered.

Leonidas stood and spun slowly, looking all around the dim space. It was empty.

"There's no blood on the floor," Jasim said. "There was at Adams's place. From having the implants cut out." He scratched his jaw. "Did he dodge the drone's attack? And then flee, figuring it wasn't safe to come back home?"

"Fleeing isn't likely for a cyborg," Leonidas said, giving him a quick frown.

Jasim frowned back. Was that an implication that he thought *Jasim* would flee in a tough situation? He had never run away during a fight. Just because he'd wanted to leave the military…that didn't mean people couldn't depend on him in a skirmish.

"If he woke up in time to dodge," Leonidas said, prodding the blanket on the floor with his armored foot, "why wouldn't he have simply destroyed the drone? It wasn't that hard to put it out of commission."

"I don't know, sir."

Jasim headed back to the office, thinking there might be something enlightening on the netdisc. He tapped at it, but it wanted a passcode or retina match, and he had neither.

A couple of minutes later, Leonidas walked in, holding something between his gauntleted thumb and index finger.

"Is that a needle?" Jasim asked.

"With a suspicious substance on the end, yes."

"Poison."

"I found the needle on the floor by the bed. We'd have to get it analyzed to know for sure that there's poison on it, and to see if it's a match for the substance Yumi examined. I don't know if we'll find a lab here where you can drop something off for study."

"A police lab on a core planet could do it, but I doubt the mafia-owned enforcer outfits here spend much time bothering with forensic studies."

"Doubtful," Leonidas said, but he walked into the kitchen and found a small container to seal it in. "Unless this simply fell out, it looks like those drones can *fire* their needles." He touched the side of his neck, perhaps remembering the battle on the station and thinking he had been closer to becoming a pincushion than he'd realized.

"I didn't see a needle left behind when I found Adams. Just a tiny hole in his neck."

"Maybe someone came and took it out to remove the evidence. Or maybe they're not actually supposed to be launched, just stabbed and withdrawn."

"I don't know, but I'm seeing a good case for starting to sleep in our combat armor."

Leonidas nodded. "That might not be a bad warning to send out to everyone. I've slept in mine before."

"Because enemies were flinging poisonous darts at you?"

"Because it lets me lock myself down so I don't lash out in my sleep." Leonidas's lips twisted wryly, but there wasn't any humor in his eyes.

"Nightmares?" Jasim said, thinking of the headband Leonidas had mentioned. He would have to look for one of those one day.

"Yes." Leonidas waved the container. "We'll see if we can get this analyzed somewhere, but I don't want to delay checking on the address your skip tracer gave us. The longer it takes us to find him, the more likely he'll be ready and waiting for us. And he *has* to be stopped. There's no honor in this."

"Yes, sir," Jasim agreed quietly.

Honor wasn't what he worried about. He just didn't want to be killed in his sleep. No, he realized, thinking again of those who had died, men he had known. It wasn't just about him. If it had been, he wouldn't have called Leonidas to help. He wanted to keep the cyborgs in his old unit from being killed, from being hunted to extinction. He'd never truly felt like he fit into the unit or into the military in general, but he still felt a kinship toward those men. They'd fought and bled together, suffered in both victory and defeat, and against all odds, they had survived the fall of the empire. He didn't want them to be killed now for nothing. He also did not want to become the last of his kind.

CHAPTER NINE

Wind whistled across the desert, sand pinging off Jasim's armor. He and Leonidas stood atop a hill, looking down at a single building on the outer edge of the outskirts of Port Thorn. A road sign proclaimed it simply, "The Cantina." A place, apparently, for those who couldn't be bothered to travel that last quarter mile to experience a wider variety of options. Or maybe for those who would be shot if they showed up in the city.

Jasim eyed the pitted and cracked stone stairs leading down to the open doors of the partially underground structure. Though one of the suns still burned in the sky, the raucous laughter and shouts coming through those doors, rising over the thumping of thunderous music, hinted of a big crowd. The stone walls had recently been painted white, but the faint outline of dark graffiti was still visible underneath. Hover cars, small aircraft, and thrust bikes were parked on the flat roof of the building, and as Jasim watched, a couple of drunken men struggled to maneuver up the steps to their vehicle. One paused to vomit over the railing.

"An auspicious looking establishment," Jasim said.

"Your contact said this is where Terrance Dufour gets his mail?" Leonidas said, not deigning to comment on the auspiciousness of the building. "It doesn't look much like a post office."

"McCall said it was the only address she could dig up. One does wonder why, if our killer lives nearby, he waited to attack Banding. His shop is only a few miles away. Why would Dufour, or someone he hired, murder cyborgs on other planets first? What would be the significance of going alphabetically down the list?"

"Aside from the fact that we're both overdue for a visit?"

"I'm trying not to think about that," Jasim said. "As I'm wearing my full armor, helmet, and snuggly neck piece for more reasons than the sand."

"Let's go in and see if anyone knows anything."

"We don't even have a description for him." Jasim had looked up the man's name after McCall had provided it and this address, but the sys-net hadn't had anything on him. He either lived off the grid completely, or that was a fake name. Jasim hoped it wasn't a fake address.

"Maybe we'll just listen to conversations and hope we hear people making dastardly plans concerning cyborgs."

"We could hear that in any Alliance-friendly bar. We didn't have to come all the way to Dustor for it." Jasim smiled, hoping he wouldn't sound like he was complaining, even if he was. When he had signed up for the cyborg surgery, he'd thought the idea of being faster and stronger sounded wonderful—nobody would ever pick on him again. He hadn't thought he'd be treated like the monster in some old fairy tale.

Leonidas's only response was to grunt and head down the slope toward the cantina.

"Sorry, sir," Jasim said, jogging to catch up.

Leonidas looked at him.

"For complaining," Jasim clarified. "I shouldn't. I should be stoic and just accept what the suns hand me. I always remember that after the complaint comes out."

Leonidas paused before going down the steps. "You should be stoic, accept the ramifications of your choices, but fight like the three hells for what you want in this universe." He continued down the stairs without waiting for a response.

It took Jasim a moment to kick his legs back into motion.

"Imperials!" someone cried as soon as Leonidas stepped across the threshold.

"Cyborgs!" someone else blurted.

Neither of those cries rang with joyous enthusiasm, so Jasim hurried up to come in beside Leonidas. Judging by the greeting, they might have to endure a bar fight before finding out any information.

The music halted with a thump and an electronic squeal. Men and women rushed to a back door, knocking over tables and chairs—and each other—as they went. Some of the waitstaff fled in the same direction, the smoky air swirling around them. Footsteps sounded on the roof as people raced to their vehicles. Others sprinted out into the desert without looking back.

"I guess they didn't see my stickers," Leonidas said.

"Nobody ever sees anything except the intimidating armor—and the intimidating man underneath. That's why I couldn't get a normal job after I finished my degree." Jasim waved toward the now-empty chairs and the fallen tables. A few indifferent souls remained at their tables in the shadows, not appearing alarmed, but even they watched Leonidas and Jasim warily.

"You went to school after the war?" Leonidas sounded surprised. "What did you get your degree in?"

"Education. With a minor in psychology."

Leonidas looked at him oddly. Yes, those weren't natural choices for an imperial cyborg. And this probably wasn't the time to discuss it further.

"I wanted to teach," was all Jasim said, and shrugged.

A throat cleared behind the bar where a man and an android had been mixing drinks. The human appeared far more exasperated than the android, who continued to fulfill orders even though it was unlikely those who had placed them would return for them.

"I hope you two are planning to order a lot of drinks," the man said, his bald head gleaming under the artificial lights, "because you just drove away the majority of my customers."

"We're looking for someone," Jasim said.

"Imagine my shock."

Roars came from above as hovercraft and aircraft took off. The bartender sighed. Or maybe he was the owner. If so, he might know about Dufour.

Jasim looked at Leonidas, expecting he would take the lead, but he started walking around the bar, looking down hallways and opening doors.

"Are you the owner?" Jasim asked, walking up to the bar.

"Stop that," the bartender said, swatting the android. "They're not coming back for those, and you're wasting good alcohol. If you need something to do, set those tables and chairs upright. And if any cyborgs harass me, get in their way, so I can make an escape."

"Harass, sir?" the android asked, setting down a bottle of green liquor. "Harass: apply aggressive pressure or intimidation, sometimes in a sexual manner."

"*Especially* get in the way if sexual manners are deployed," the barkeeper grumbled, waving the android toward the furniture. He turned to Jasim. "I better not be who you're looking for. This place is legitimate, and I never had any trouble with the empire when it was in power, *not* that it's in power anymore." He gave Jasim's armor a pointed look. "You there, Cyborg Number Two, this isn't a tourist zone."

"Two?" Leonidas had stepped through a doorway and was looking at something in a room in the back.

"He's Cyborg Number One," Jasim said. "Definitely."

"I don't care if you're twins that were fused together at birth. I'd appreciate it if you'd both leave so my clients will come back. Oh, and if you want to drop a few hundred tindarks on the bar here, that *might* cover what I'm losing right now."

"This looks like a mini post office back here," Leonidas murmured, the words quiet enough that the barkeeper shouldn't hear them.

"I didn't catch your name," Jasim said to the bartender while wriggling a couple of fingers in Leonidas's direction. "I'm going to assume you're not the person we're looking for, or you would be more nervous right now."

"I'm *positive* I'm not the person you're looking for."

Jasim debated whether he should mention Dufour. The bartender might have a way to comm him and warn him that cyborgs were looking for him.

"Back here, Jasim," Leonidas said quietly.

The bartender glared in his direction.

"What's back there?" Jasim asked, though he doubted he was going to get any information from the man, not without applying force, at which point the android would step in. Then they would end up wrecking the establishment in the fight that ensued. That wouldn't do anything to improve cyborg-local relations.

"Your ugly buddy." The man grabbed a towel, pointedly wiped down the bar, and ignored both of them.

Jasim started toward the back room, but Leonidas came out. He set a small stack of Alliance tindarks on the top of the bar in front of the man, the holograms on the paper bills gleaming.

"Terrance Dufour," Leonidas said, pitching his voice so the patrons wouldn't hear it. "Are you familiar with him?"

The bartender eyed him suspiciously, but did count the bills the best he could with Leonidas's hand atop the stack.

"He may rent a box here." The man waved to the room Leonidas had been in. "A lot of people do. Post office doesn't deliver out in the Dunes."

"And that's where he lives?"

The bartender shrugged. "I don't ask where people live. It's ten tindarks a month to rent a box, no questions asked. And no explosives allowed to be delivered. But I trust people on that one. I don't search their mail. I run an honest business."

"How often does Dufour come to check his box?" Leonidas asked.

Another shrug. "A couple of times a week, either him, if he wants a drink, or one of his drones."

"Mail been delivered today?"

"A while ago, yeah."

"What's his box number?"

"I don't know. It's on the far end, I think. Second row from the top."

"You think?"

"I'm *positive*. How many questions do I have to answer before I can pocket your bribe?"

Leonidas stared at the man long enough to make him squirm, then lifted his hand and walked back into the post office room. The bartender slid the money into his pocket, but he turned a disgruntled expression on Jasim.

"You're not going to set up camp back there, are you?"

"We won't have to if you tell us where the man lives." Jasim didn't know whether it had been a good idea to tell the man who they were looking for, but there might not have been much choice if the names weren't etched on the boxes back there.

"I said I don't know," the bartender growled.

"And you wouldn't know how to get in contact with him to warn him that a couple of cyborgs are looking for him?"

"Definitely not."

Jasim didn't believe him. Maybe he ought to rethink the application of force. He supposed it wouldn't be polite to brutalize a man they had just bribed, but it wouldn't be that odd on Dustor.

"Jasim," Leonidas said from the back room.

After checking to make sure neither the android nor the remaining customers appeared to be planning anything shifty, Jasim joined him.

It was a larger room than he expected, with stairs leading up to some upper level, a short hallway going straight back to the kitchen, and a large open area to the right with lockers lining two long walls. A wide door was closed at the end. Some of the patrons had probably fled that way.

"If the bartender is honest, this is the box," Leonidas said, touching the indicated one. Judging by the front, it was large enough to accept packages as well as envelopes.

"It wouldn't be wise of him to be dishonest when we're here and Dufour isn't."

"No."

"So we just have to loiter here to see if he comes by for his mail in the next couple of days?" Jasim grimaced, knowing Maddy wouldn't appreciate it if this side trip took numerous days—or more. He also doubted the owner would let them lurk back here indefinitely. He would either have his android try to throw them out, or he would call in someone with more firepower.

"Why don't you open it and see if there's mail waiting?" Leonidas said. "If there is, he might have gotten an alert and come sooner rather than later." He pointed toward the front room. "I'll watch the owner, make sure he's not sending any warning messages."

"I wouldn't think of doing such a thing," the bartender said, poking his head through the doorway. "It would be bad for my health. And you've already paid me more than he has in a year of renting a box here." He smiled and strode through the post room and into the kitchen.

"He's lying," Jasim said, finding that smile insincere. The rest of him too.

"Yes," Leonidas said, waving his fingers toward the mailboxes.

Jasim took a spot in front of the right one. A simple physical lock opened by a key held the dented metal door shut. With his strong fingers, it would have been easy enough to break the box open, but he'd brought a lock-picking kit too. The Pulverizer preferred for his workers to repossess people's belongings without damaging anything. Apparently, that was better for business.

Jasim affixed the magnetic device over the lock and tapped a button to set it to work. Leonidas disappeared up the stairs. Snooping? Jasim was surprised. He would have expected his old commander to tend toward being blunt and straightforward. The bribe also surprised him. Most cyborgs used force to get what they wanted—it was what they were good at. Besides, when they'd been enforcing imperial laws, it had usually been justified.

A click sounded, and the panel popped open. Leonidas came back down the stairs as Jasim peeked into the locker. A single package rested inside in a typical blue CargoExpress mail crate.

"Should we open it?" Jasim asked.

"It could be full of materials for killing more cyborgs," Leonidas said grimly.

"I'm not sure if that's a yes or not, sir. Or if it was a yes and that *I* should be the one to open it."

"You are the one with the lock-picking device," Leonidas said, heading over to the kitchen door and monitoring. The bartender hadn't come out yet.

"That's not required for opening mail packages," Jasim said.

He slid the little crate out, pressed his finger onto an indention, and held it until a soft *snap-hiss* sounded. The lid rose, and Jasim held the box at arm's length, prepared to stuff it back in the locker and slam the door shut if explosives waited inside. Or worse, poisons.

Nothing blew, flew, or oozed out of the crate.

He peered inside. "Uh, comic books?"

"What?" Leonidas asked, looking from the kitchen toward the box.

Jasim poked through them. "Physical copies of comics. They're all in the same series. This one's signed." He looked into the locker, half-expecting a box of poison components to still be hiding in the shadows. "Maybe our bartender friend lied to us after all."

"If he did," Leonidas spoke loudly, looking back into the kitchen, "we'll have to open all of the boxes. Forcibly."

"I didn't *lie*," came a weary reply.

Leonidas shrugged at Jasim.

Jasim shook his head and placed the comic books neatly back in the box, an uneasy thought starting to niggle at him. "It's not possible, is it…I mean, what would happen if the person we're after is a kid?"

"A kid with money to afford collectors' items? And poisons? I'm sure it's an adult."

Jasim returned the crate to the locker and closed it, doing his best to ensure it did not look like anyone had broken into it. "What now? We wait to see if he comes to pick up his package today?"

Leonidas nodded. "He'll come eventually."

"Unless he's been warned that we're here, waiting for him," Jasim said quietly, aware of glasses clinking in the kitchen.

"I'll go chat with the owner."

"Chat? Will his android get involved?"

"Possibly," Leonidas said. "Though I assure you, a sexual manner won't be applied."

"That assurance wasn't really necessary, sir."

"Good. Go find a spot outside where we can keep an eye on that door."

"Yes, sir."

CHAPTER TEN

Plants were not in great abundance on this part of Dustor, and the sandy landscape outside of the cantina did not offer many hidden places from which to spy upon it. Jasim climbed back up the slope they had originally descended and managed to find the remains of a corner of a centuries-old building, the crumbling wall standing about three feet high. The spot was visible from the crossroads, but he doubted many people would zip over to investigate it. He crouched down behind the wall and took his helmet off so that if he peered back toward the cantina, a bright red blob would not draw anyone's eye.

Minutes dribbled past as Jasim waited for Leonidas to come outside. Far fewer vehicles were parked on the roof of the cantina now, but the second sun was setting, and Jasim wagered business would pick up again soon. Evening might be the ideal time for someone to come by and pick up mail while grabbing a drink. Or evening three days from now. He grimaced.

If Dufour *did* show up, how would they know him from other patrons? Would he head straight for that post office entrance instead of going in through the front door? Would he be alone instead of in a crowd? Would he look like the beady-eyed, nefarious sort who murdered innocent cyborgs?

Jasim's helmet comm beeped, and he winced, knowing who it would be without looking. Who else on Dustor had a reason to talk to him?

"Yes, Maddy?" he answered.

"How much longer is this errand of yours going to take?" she asked without preamble. "I got a message from my son-in-law. He wants us to hurry to our next assignment. The owners have increased what they're offering to pay for those ships' return."

"Did Leonidas not arrange for a handsome young man to entertain you while we're out here?" Jasim had foisted that research on Leonidas, having a notion that since he was married, he would know more about picking out a nice prostitute for a woman. It was possible that was faulty logic, but he certainly hadn't had a clue about shopping for such things.

"Yes, he did, but I don't need to be entertained for days."

"I'll try to expedite things," Jasim said, as if he knew how to do so. Unless their target was itching for those comic books and came to get them that day, he and Leonidas could spend a long time watching this building. "Maddy, when you're done with your, uhm, visitor, why don't you bring the *Interrogator* over to the Red Dunes Cantina? I'll buy you and your friend a drink."

"I can't believe you're bribing me to stay on this dustball."

"It might be a good idea to have you close if we need to chase someone down."

"Chase…Listen, kid. I'm not here to chase people unless they're piloting stolen goods that we've been hired to retrieve. Dustor isn't a good place to pick fights with people. You never know who they'll end up being connected to."

"Just come by, please," Jasim said. "We may need you."

Maddy grumbled and cut the comm. Jasim wasn't sure if that signaled agreement or not. He thought it would be a good idea to have the ship close in case Dufour arrived in a ship of his own. Jasim and Leonidas could take out just about any foe on foot, but even cyborgs had trouble wrestling armed and armored spaceships to the ground.

A few minutes later, Leonidas appeared, walking up the back stairs and away from the cantina. He was alone. Jasim waved him up the hill and to the wall.

"You convinced the owner not to comm Dufour?" Jasim asked.

"I convinced the owner to tell his android to tend the bar and then lock himself in his own lavatory for a while."

"Huh, I didn't know you were that convincing."

"Brute force was involved. Sometimes it's the easiest way to accomplish something."

"Yes, sir. I wasn't judging you."

"No?" Leonidas asked, crouching behind the wall with Jasim. "What is it you do with a psychology degree?"

"That was my minor. I majored in education. I wanted to be a counselor or maybe a coach or a teacher and help young people," Jasim said, watching him out of the side of his eye, expecting him to scoff. "I especially wanted to work with kids. Because when I was a kid...well, I didn't have anyone to go to for advice. I would have liked to have had someone."

Leonidas, facing the cantina, did not answer.

"I know, maybe it's a waste of all those implants," Jasim said, feeling the need to explain, to make someone understand—the suns knew those hiring firms hadn't. "But I...well, I wasn't one of the ones who enjoyed the fighting. I guess that's not a secret to you on account of...my meeting with you. I did it, and I shot those who opposed us because we had to or they'd shoot us, but when I joined up, I was just looking for a way off the streets. And the bonus they gave us for agreeing to the cyborg upgrades...I'd never thought I'd see that much money in my life. It paid for almost all of my schooling. I've just got a few small loans left I'm paying off. But more than that, I confess, at the time, I just wanted to make sure I'd never be picked on again, never be the scrawny street rat running from bullies."

Jasim cleared his throat and looked out toward the desert. This was more personal information—more *honesty*—than he'd meant to share. Especially while they were out here on a stakeout of a mailbox.

"Anyway," he said, "I'm just wanting to do something...useful with my degree. After destroying—killing—so many in the war, some of whom I wasn't sure we should be killing, I'd like to make up for it in a way. I know that's not really possible, but at least if I could help people now...maybe it would make a small difference."

"Why aren't you?" Leonidas asked.

Jasim couldn't tell from his tone if he was curious or if he cared at all—or if he thought Jasim was being a wuss.

"I applied to a lot of places after I finished school. As soon as people found out my history—what I was—they made excuses to cancel my interviews. Or they invited me in only to tell me that nobody was going to hire a cyborg to work with kids."

Leonidas straightened slightly, peering over the wall. "The post office is getting a visitor."

Jasim leaned around the crumbled end of the wall as a round, floating drone with antennae extending from the top and articulating arms protruding from its belly flew toward the back of the cantina. This one was silver instead of bronze, but it reminded him of the other drone.

The back door opened, and it floated inside.

"If our target sent a drone to pick up the mail, keeping up with it may not be a simple matter," Leonidas said.

"We could shoot it down," Jasim said.

"Then it wouldn't lead us back to Dufour."

"Good point."

Further, a drone could fly out of the range of their weapons quickly.

"Have you talked to your pilot recently?" Leonidas asked.

"Yes." Jasim didn't mention the reason for that conversation. "She should already be on her way."

"Good. Make sure of that, and tell her to hurry. Following a drone in a ship would be—"

He stopped speaking when the door opened again. The round drone zipped out and up the stairs with a familiar blue mail package clasped in its grippers. It beelined straight out toward the Dune Sea. Quickly.

"Comm the pilot," Leonidas said, jumping to his feet and over the wall. "I'll keep it in sight, and you can track my armor, pick me up, and we'll keep following it."

He was already running away before he finished speaking, his legs churning as he raced after the drone. Jasim had no idea what its top speed would be, but tapped his comm unit to comply. He wagered it could fly faster than a cyborg could run, even one whose already enhanced speed was further enhanced by combat armor.

"Maddy?" Jasim asked. "I need a pick up, right now."

The drone had already disappeared from his sight. He hoped Leonidas, who was speeding over the first of the dunes, could keep it in sight. Jasim wished he'd thought to bring a tracking device along. This would have been much easier if they had stuck a beacon to the bottom of that package.

"What happened to my drink?" Maddy replied.

"I'll buy you two after we run this errand. Hurry, please."

Grumbling came over the comm. Jasim paced behind the wall and looked back toward the city, hoping to spot the *Interrogator* flying over the skyline.

Fortunately, Maddy was dependable, even if she groused while being dependable. The ship soon appeared, tracking his comm and arrowing toward him.

"Don't land," Jasim said, jogging away from the wall. "Just hover and open the hatch. I'll jump in." He looked toward the desert again, but Leonidas and the drone were out of sight now.

The sleek ship swooped low, its logo glinting in the setting sun. It hovered twenty meters away from Jasim, kicking up sand that railed against his armor. As soon as the hatch opened, he ran and sprang ten feet into the air. He landed on the threshold, tugged the hatch shut, and sprinted into NavCom.

"Head out into the dunes," he ordered, stepping over the knitting basket and sliding into the co-pilot's seat. A half-finished project lay on the console in front of him. He pushed it aside and networked his armor with the *Interrogator's* modest sensor station, using the comm link he had with Leonidas to locate his suit. "We're going there." He pointed as a holodisplay popped up, showing a blip for his location.

"I was almost done with my project, you know," Maddy said, giving him a dark look.

"Leonidas's hat?"

"His tassels. I'm going to use the rainbow yarn to make them extra colorful."

"I'm sure his children will like that." Jasim leaned forward, as if he could urge the ship to go faster just with his body. "Where's your gentleman caller? Did he not want to stay for a drink?"

"He made a snide comment about my age, so I kicked him off the ship early."

"Ah, unfortunate."

"Yes, it is. He's lucky I didn't lodge one of my needles up his ass. Next time, I'll take longer picking one from a catalog."

"Maybe you should try going on dates instead," Jasim said. That was what normal people did to find mates, wasn't it? He'd never had much of an opportunity to try before entering the Cyborg Corps. In the neighborhood where he had grown up, "dates" had usually involved running from mafia hoodlums with a girl one liked or trying not to get shot while sitting on a moonlit rooftop and gazing out over a cityscape.

"Hard to date when you're on a different planet every week," Maddy said.

Jasim eyed the blip as they drew closer and tried to spot Leonidas on the view screen. That blip was still moving, so he must not have lost track of the drone yet.

"Maybe you could retire and settle down on one planet for a while," he said as he tapped the sensors, hoping to locate the drone itself. Such a small device would normally be hard to spot, but with nothing but sand underneath them and the city fading to the rear, they should be able to find it. Or so he thought. The dunes looked empty of homes and machinery of any sort, but the sensors showed otherwise. Buildings were built into the dunes, and here and there, equipment sent out signals. Those signals clogged the sensors, and he ended up growling as he struggled to pick out the tiny drone in the mess.

"Retire?" Maddy asked. "From flying? Are you daft?"

"Occasionally." Jasim pointed. "There's Leonidas."

"*That's* who we're chasing? You being all noble-hearted, I figured we were after evildoers."

"*He's* after evildoers. But we're picking him up and continuing the quest."

"Let's see if I can even catch him," Maddy said, dipping lower to the desert floor. "Damn, he's fast. You cyborgs are freaks."

She didn't say it with any rancor—occasionally, Jasim even had the sense that Maddy liked him—but the words filled him with a sense of bleakness. What did it mean that even allies thought of them as something less than human?

"Is he going to jump in, or do we have to bowl him over?" Maddy asked.

Jasim commed Leonidas. "We're right behind you."

"I'm aware," Leonidas said, his breathing hard.

"And…" Jasim let out a soft, triumphant "hah" as the sensors finally picked up the drone ahead of Leonidas. He locked onto it so they wouldn't lose it. "We've got the drone in our sights, sir. Stop so we can get you."

Leonidas slowed at the top of a dune, though he continued to look off toward the horizon instead of at the ship zipping toward him, as if he didn't trust Jasim not to lose his target. Maddy hit the button to open the hatch and flew over him.

"Hop up, sir," Jasim said.

"Hop up, he says about a twenty-foot leap," Maddy muttered.

A clang sounded from the corridor behind them, Leonidas's boots landing on the deck. Maddy shut the hatch and took off after the drone. Jasim leaned forward again, willing it to come onto the view screen and wondering how far out into the desert it would lead them. What was the range on those little drones? Fifty miles? A hundred?

Maddy picked up speed, and they closed on it. Finally, it came into sight. Jasim almost laughed at the metallic ball floating across the dunes with the perky blue package in its grip. He was surprised someone didn't pop up from behind a dune and shoot it for its prize. But the number of buried buildings and equipment was dwindling as they flew farther from the city. Jasim couldn't imagine where the delivery was going. He wondered if the drone sensed that it was being followed and was taking them on a chase.

"Stay back a little," he told Maddy. "We don't want it to be nervous about how close we're stalking it."

"A nervous drone?"

"We also don't want to fly over a dune, run into a huge fortress full of artillery weapons, and get shot down," he added, though the sensors should have told him if anything of that magnitude lay ahead.

Leonidas stepped into NavCom, his helmet under his arm, his damp hair plastered to his head. His mouth was open as he took deep breaths, but his eyes had that gleam in them again, as if he'd enjoyed chasing that drone, like a hound after a rabbit.

"Invigorating jog, sir?" Jasim asked, as the drone flew down the backside of a dune ahead of them and dropped out of sight. It was still on the sensors, so he didn't worry.

"Next time, you get to run."

"I figured you wanted a chance to prove how fit and virile you still are, despite your increasing…maturity."

Leonidas's eyes narrowed. He might have said something, but a plaintive bleep came from the sensors.

"Uh," Jasim said, looking from the panel to the sand ahead as the *Interrogator* flew over the dune the drone had gone down. It had disappeared from the sensors.

"Where did it go?" Maddy asked, toggling between the ship's various exterior cameras.

"I'm not reading it anymore," Jasim said slowly. "But that doesn't make any sense. It couldn't have flown out of range that quickly."

He looked toward Leonidas, thinking he might have an answer.

Leonidas shook his head, gazing at the view screen and the miles and miles of sand and dunes that stretched away beneath the red sky. The empty devoid-of-drones miles.

"We'll have to get out and search," Jasim said. "It must have gone to ground. But it should still show up on the sensors if that were the case." After all, they had been picking up all manner of underground facilities earlier.

"It might have flown into a compound that has shielding from sensors," Leonidas said.

"No search." Maddy spun in her chair to face Jasim. "I've gone along with this little side trip, because you're nice boys, and you brought me yarn and a man, but we can't stay on Dustor indefinitely."

"We're not planning to search indefinitely, Maddy," Jasim said.

"It's a tiny drone somewhere out there under miles and miles of sand. The saying about needles and haystacks comes to mind."

"It couldn't have gone far in that little bit of time," Jasim said.

"It could still take you days to find it. And I've had my son-in-law nagging me on the comm. As he's been pointing out, he loses money when this ship isn't flying jobs. He loses even *more* money when it's burning fuel on a planet it shouldn't even be on. It's time for the *Interrogator* and its *crew*—" she gave Jasim a pointed look, "—to go back to work."

"I…need to do this, Maddy," Jasim said.

"Then you're going to get bumped off the crew."

He looked at her bleakly. Couldn't he have a few days to help his kind without losing his job? "Can't you at least wait until dawn?"

Maddy hit a button on the comm panel, and The Pulverizer's familiar face appeared, dark eyes angry, tattooed cheek twitching, his sharp jaw made sharper by the trimmed beard that outlined its contours.

"What is my ship doing on *Dustor*?" he demanded, the message recorded earlier. "Maddy, what are you doing? Having a honeymoon with that cyborg? You think I have so many ships in my fleet that I can have some of them going off on sightseeing tours? I want the *Interrogator* back here, with the cyborg or without—someone's going out to get these yachts. Damn it, Maddy, this is a big deal, and that's *my* ship you've absconded with. You *will* return it." The Pulverizer slapped his hand down to close the comm.

"He's more polite with you than he is with me," Jasim observed. "He uses your first name."

"If I don't answer him soon, that'll change," Maddy grumbled.

"I brought some rat bars," Leonidas said. "We can search and make it back to the city on foot on our own if need be."

Jasim grimaced. "I'm sure we could, but…this is my *job*. And jobs aren't easy to come by." He had no delusions about The Pulverizer rehiring him if he simply disappeared, going off on this personal mission. Maybe it was foolish to think that it wasn't already too late. He might lose his job because of the choice he'd already made, because he had bribed Maddy to fly so far out of the way. Even though he longed to do something else with his life, it wasn't as if he could simply go out and start a career as a teacher when he finished here. He'd already tried that. And if The Pulverizer put out a warning about his lack of reliability, would he even be able to get another job in this business?

"*I'll* go search then," Leonidas said, and stalked back to the hatch.

A faint hiss sounded as it unsealed, and he soon appeared walking along the side of the dune underneath them.

"Let him finish this," Maddy said. "Whatever it is."

Jasim sighed and stood up. "I can't. I'm the one who asked him for help with this."

"I can't wait for you."

"I know. I understand." He rested a hand on her shoulder. She'd already detoured far from their itinerary to bring him here. "Thanks and good luck with your next partner."

"Partner?" Maddy's eyebrows rose. "Whoever told you that you were my partner? You're just the hired meat." She smiled as she said the words and swatted him on the back with a knitting needle as he left NavCom.

He couldn't manage a return smile, not with his future looking bleak. But it would be much bleaker if they didn't stop this killer.

CHAPTER ELEVEN

The last sun had set, the stars gleaming in the sky overhead, so Jasim paused in his pacing to put on his helmet and allow his armor's night-vision powers to amplify his sight. Cyborgs had optical enhancements to see in dim conditions, but he didn't want to chance missing anything. Jasim and Leonidas had already been walking around the side and base of the long dune for an hour. He was about to head into the valley between it and another long dune to broaden the search area. He doubted the drone could have gone far in the time between when they had last seen it flying over that dune and when they'd flown over it themselves.

Leonidas did not speak much, and Jasim found himself missing Maddy's commentary, even if she would have mocked them for simply kicking sand around down here. The *Interrogator* had disappeared as soon as they had jumped out, leaving them alone out here. After only an hour, Jasim wouldn't let himself believe they were wasting their time, but he couldn't help but wonder what he would do if they found nothing. If they had to walk back to Port Thorn empty-handed. If they were able to stop the killer, losing his job would be worth it, but if not…

"I think it makes most sense that something would be *in* one of these dunes," Leonidas said, crouching and sweeping at something in the sand. "A structure below could have caused a dune to form, or the dune itself could be a manmade object."

"Yes," Jasim said, joining him and putting more effort into poking into and sweeping away sand. "And you would think a garage door or whatever opened up for the drone couldn't be buried too deeply."

"There aren't any vehicle tracks anywhere. Dufour either flies to and from his mail delivery spot, or the sand shifts to cover tracks quickly."

"Dustor is a hard place to track someone."

Jasim patted and thumped at the slope, freezing when one of the thumps sounded hollow. He swept away sand, or tried to. In this spot, the sand did not act normally. It was as if it was glued together. Maybe it was.

He continued patting around the area, trying to find a crack or outline of a door. "Want to help me, sir?"

Leonidas had climbed to the top of the dune and was looking out into the desert. Jasim's first thought was that Maddy might have changed her mind and was heading back, but he was gazing in the opposite direction from the city. Nothing but miles and miles of sand and dunes lay out there.

"You see the owner coming home to get his comic books?" Jasim asked.

"No." Leonidas hustled down the side of the dune, sand sliding under his boots. "Not unless he's been out carousing with a hundred other people."

"A hundred?" Jasim stood up, but from his spot, he couldn't see through the next dune and to whatever—whoever—Leonidas had seen.

"A dozen open hovercraft are heading this way, all with armed people in them. Desert pirates, would be my guess, maybe heading to town to visit the cantina."

"So long as they're not coming to visit us." Jasim had confidence in his and Leonidas's fighting abilities, but fifty to one odds were not good, even for a cyborg. Those hovercraft might have anti-personnel weapons mounted on them.

"I'd suggest we take cover under something, but…" Leonidas spread a hand, indicating the distinct lack of cover.

"If we hunker over by that dune, they won't have much time to see us as they fly over." Jasim hoped the darkness would help further, but the hovercraft would probably have lights.

"Let's do it." Leonidas took off, running fast again.

Jasim hurried to catch up, hearing the first sounds of the approaching craft, the rumble of engines and churning of propeller fans. He and Leonidas reached the dune and sat down with their backs to it. Jasim draped an arm over his knee. They were just two cyborgs relaxing out in the desert. No reason for pirates to stop and harass them.

"Should we take off our helmets to appear less like we're looking for a fight?" Jasim asked.

"Whether we're looking for one or not, it'll probably come to us if they see us."

Jasim thought of the bikers on Primus 7. He wagered Dufour hadn't had to spend much to bribe them to attack cyborgs. "You're probably right."

The noise of the engines grew louder. Was it a coincidence that the hovercraft were flying on a route that would take them directly overhead? Jasim looked across to where he had been poking at the suspiciously clumped sand—nothing unusual about it was visible from here.

"Do you think our friend might have seen us out here and called for them to come visiting?" he asked.

"It's possible. Some of the people out here might also pay the pirates for protection, protection from outsiders, protection from them."

Jasim snorted. "Right."

The first hovercraft buzzed past overhead, its frame and fuel tanks visible from below. A few people's arms were dangling over the sides of the craft. Instead of hugging the ground and following the contours of the dunes, the hovercraft continued straight across, staying well above Jasim and Leonidas. Several more flew into view, dark shapes against the starry sky. A few had headlights, or perhaps search lights, in the fronts, the beams stretching ahead of the craft.

At first, it seemed like the pilots hadn't seen Jasim and Leonidas and would continue on, but the lead craft banked and descended, sweeping into the valley between the two dunes. The others followed, tattooed faces and windswept thatches of hair coming into view. Those faces were all turned toward Jasim and Leonidas.

Sighing, Jasim rose to his feet. "A fight indeed."

Leonidas also stood up, and Jasim thought he might raise his rifle to take the first shot before the pirates got closer or fully committed to anything. But he propped his fists on his hips and waited.

Soon, ten large hovercraft floated above the sand between their dune and the next, all of them facing Jasim and Leonidas. Artillery weapons were mounted on some of them, long barrels extending out over the skirts.

Jasim's suit adjusted the night vision setting so he wouldn't be blinded by the headlights shining into his eyes, but he could still see adequately. In the lead craft, a big man with brawny arms and long, wild hair stood up, propping a boot on the frame and leaning forward. Scars stretched along his arms, and Jasim stirred uneasily. He'd had incisions in very similar places when he'd received his implants. The empire had been careful enough and operated in such a way that its cyborgs weren't left with scars all over their bodies, but he'd heard of civilian surgeons not doing as good of a job. And he imagined ones willing to install implants purchased on the black market weren't the cream of the crop. Or had these implants been purchased directly from the source? Pirates paid for protection, indeed.

"That one may be trouble," Leonidas murmured to Jasim, nodding toward the brawny pirate.

Jasim doubted he would have the full range of cyborg upgrades, including enhanced hearing, but if he had given himself superhuman strength, he could be trouble in a fight, even if he wasn't wearing combat armor. None of the pirates were. Most of them wore simple trousers and vests, with bandanas, armbands, and heavy chain jewelry adorning their grimy clothes.

"I don't doubt it," Jasim murmured back.

"I'll handle him."

"Got a tip," the leader said, nodding toward them. "Heard there were a couple of suits of combat armor strolling around in the desert out here, just waiting to be turned into a pawnshop."

"I'm starting to think my days would be simpler if I walked around naked," Jasim muttered.

"And cyborg implants," a man behind the leader whispered. He had significantly thinner arms. "It's my turn to get some. I want the big one's implants."

"He's older," another said. "The littler man will have more recent ones."

"Hells, I just want some implants. So Cyclone won't be able to beat up on me all the time in the boxing ring."

"Implants won't do you any good if you're dead," Leonidas said coolly. "Continue on to the cantina and enjoy your lives."

The leader curled a lip. "The Lords of Crush don't take kindly to being ordered around by *imperials*. Never did."

"Cocky, ain't he?" one of his followers said.

"Lords of Crush?" Jasim asked.

"Witty," Leonidas said, then lowered his voice. "We'll both jump on the lead hovercraft. Fight them from inside, keep them from being able to shoot at us down here."

"Yes, sir," Jasim whispered. It wouldn't take much effort to make the ten-foot leap, and he agreed that they should be safer up there. In theory, the pirates wouldn't fire at their own craft.

The leader was giving his own orders. "Do your best not to utterly destroy their armor," he told his men. "But they'll be hard to kill, so you'll have to—"

Leonidas ran and sprang into the air, sailing straight toward the leader.

The man jumped back, grabbing a spiked club from the floor of his craft. Blazer pistols hung from his holster, but for some reason he picked that weapon.

As Jasim ran after Leonidas, planning to jump into the same hovercraft, pirates in the other ones fired. Orange and crimson blazer bolts lit up the night as they slammed into the sand all around him, more than one bouncing off his armor. He leaped into that first hovercraft. Leonidas and the homemade cyborg were already fighting, that spiked club versus Leonidas's gauntleted fists.

Jasim barreled into the unaltered men, those pointing blazer pistols at him. He threw punches, not hesitating to break bones as he knocked them over the side. The hovercraft deck rocked, and something snapped next to him. An ominous hiss sounded.

Jasim had hoped the other pirates would not fire into a hovercraft full of their allies, but blazer bolts streaked toward him and Leonidas. Jasim ducked and rolled across the deck of the craft, trying to keep them from pounding his armor. The deck tilted further, and he crashed into someone's legs. He turned it into an attack, grabbing the man around the waist and hurling him over the side. The man screamed, not from Jasim's throw but from one of his allies shooting him in the back. Excited shouts rose over the squeals of blazers.

The pirates didn't seem to care if they hit their own people. Maybe they were drugged or drunk. Or both. Their eyes glittered with hunger as several other hovercraft zoomed about, angling for better shots. How many of them believed they would get some implants? That they could cut them out of Leonidas's and Jasim's flesh and be able to slide them right into their own? If that was what their crazy leader had done, he was lucky he hadn't died from an infection.

A man screamed and lunged toward Jasim with something clutched in his hand. A grenade? Or perhaps a fluidwrap? Jasim rushed forward and knocked it out of his hand. Whatever it was, it flew toward one of the other hovercraft, eliciting alarmed shouts from those inside. Jasim grabbed the man by his vest. The pirate yelled and kicked him, but Jasim barely felt it through his armor. He threw the pirate over the side and started toward Leonidas, who was still facing off against the burly leader.

Before he made it more than a step, another hovercraft rammed into theirs. Jasim stumbled, the deck already tilted alarmingly. He spread his legs, planting himself and fired one of his arm blazers at the pilot ramming them. It splashed off an invisible barrier a foot in front of the man's face. Personal forcefield. Either that, or he had Starseer talents. The man grinned wildly and came in to ram them again. Several pirates behind him unloaded their blazers, the bolts streaking toward Jasim.

He dropped to his knees, using the frame of the hovercraft for cover as he returned fire. This time, he aimed for the hovercraft skirt, hoping to deflate the air cushions. They were not armored or guarded by the forcefield, and he gave a tight, satisfied smile as his blazer cut into them. Air gushed out, and the craft lurched forward, the pilot stumbling across the controls. As they struggled to brace themselves, Jasim took down three more pirates. Then the craft dropped out of view, smoke wafting from something in the rear.

Something bumped into Jasim's back, and he whirled, expecting another pirate. Right behind him, Leonidas gripped the leader and threw him over the side. Before Jasim could say anything, Leonidas leaped after him, and the two resumed wrestling before they even hit the sand.

Jasim tried to reach the pilot of the craft he was on as two other vehicles veered toward the fighters below. Someone threw something toward the men. A grenade? Jasim sucked in an alarmed breath and lunged to the side of the craft so he could shoot it before it landed. Would these fools take out their own leader just to get Leonidas? Or maybe they wouldn't hesitate to cut out their boss's implants too.

"Look out, sir," Jasim blurted.

His blazer bolt clipped the flying grenade but didn't blow it up, only altered its path slightly. It hit the dune and rolled toward the combatants.

Leonidas gripped the cyborg pirate by both arms, taking several powerful punches to his chest plate while he hefted the man from his feet. He spun and hurled him toward the grenade. Leonidas sprang away, diving and rolling down the dune. The pirate landed on the grenade as it exploded. A shriek of pain broke the desert night, but it was short-lived, as pieces of the man flew everywhere.

The horror should have scared the pirates, given them a reason to pause, but they did not even seem to care. Three craft bumped each other in their eagerness to fly after Leonidas, who was leaping to his feet at the bottom of the dune. Men opened fire on him.

Jasim had knocked all the pirates on his craft over the sides, including the pilot, but eight craft remained. He slammed a fist into the propeller fan to break it before taking a running leap toward the next closest group of pirates. He landed in the back of their craft and charged into some of the men firing on Leonidas.

Leonidas leaped into one of the hovercraft coming at him, once again dropping himself into the middle of the men, confusing everyone as he flung people about. Jasim worked on clearing his own craft. He knocked people aside, not slowing even though his armor kept getting clipped by blazer bolts. He did his best to keep men around him as shields—his armor wouldn't protect him indefinitely. Alarms flashed on his faceplate, reporting damage to his suit.

He flung a pirate into the open fan blades of the propeller, and the man screamed. Once again, Jasim wondered if the pirates were drugged. Surely, sane and sober men wouldn't keep fighting after seeing their leader blown up.

An explosion boomed from the craft Leonidas was on. Smoke flooded the sky, and his and the other hovercraft around him disappeared into the gray haze. Flames burst through, rising above the smoke cloud and licking the sky.

Someone behind Jasim shouted in surprise. At first, he thought it was because of the explosion, but then a second boom rattled the night. A shadow flew over Jasim's head, blotting out the stars. He cursed, even as he ducked more weapons fire from the hovercraft next to him. Did the pirates have reinforcements? Men in airplanes or spacecraft? If so, those would be much harder to bring down.

But as he rolled to his feet to throw another man overboard, he recognized the vessel zooming down, parting the smoke. The *Interrogator*.

The forward e-cannon blazed blue as the ship fired. The energy blast struck down, and a hovercraft snapped in half, wreckage flying. The two pieces hit the sand and skidded down the dune.

Finally, the pirates seemed to realize and accept that they were outnumbered. The four craft that remained serviceable turned away from the battle, wobbling and bobbing as they headed toward the horizon. Jasim, not wanting to see the pirates again, decided to take down the one he was aboard instead of letting it escape. The more blows they landed, the better.

He tore the propeller casing from the deck and hurled it into the dune. It struck hard, metal screeching as broken blades flew across the sand. The hovercraft pitched sideways under his feet, and he leaped free of it.

He landed on his feet in the sand, his arms extended, the blazers in his suit ready to fire, but the battle was over. Smoke wafted from six wrecked craft around him, and the pirates who had been thrown overboard, the ones who were conscious and could move, were running or hobbling away.

Jasim spotted Leonidas a hundred meters away with the *Interrogator* settling down in the sand behind him. After making sure none of the downed pirates around him looked like they would make more trouble, Jasim headed toward Leonidas.

He opened a comm channel to the *Interrogator*. "Thought you were leaving us, Maddy."

"I was, but I realized I hadn't finished your friend's hat yet."

"Ah."

"Also, I was scanning the channels of the local authorities and heard them talking about trouble in the desert, trouble that they decided wasn't close enough to the city to worry about. I just had a feeling you were at the source of it."

"I don't know why you would assume that," Jasim said. "We're law-abiding and gentle souls."

Leonidas had removed his helmet, and he lifted his eyebrows at this statement. "You must not have told her about the cantina owner that we locked in his own lav."

"*You* did that, sir. All I did was—"

"Illegally open someone's mail?"

Jasim held a finger to his lips over his faceplate. "Shh, she can hear you saying those things. She might not finish knitting your hat if she learns what a miscreant you are."

"That would be a tragedy," Leonidas murmured, turning to face the slope where Jasim had been digging earlier.

"What did he say?" Maddy asked. "I didn't hear that."

"He said that however many tassels you're adding to his hat, it's not enough. Cyborgs *love* tassels."

Leonidas squinted at him, but did not comment. He strode toward the slope with the suspiciously clumped sand. Jasim gawked at the smoke wafting from his charred and dented armor. It would need a lot of repair time in his case and likely an extended visit with an armor smith. His own was probably smoking just as much.

He hoped that whatever waited inside that dune wouldn't cause too much trouble, but he had a feeling that was a delusional hope.

CHAPTER TWELVE

Leonidas slid a gauntleted hand along the outline of what he believed to be a hidden door in the side of the dune. It might simply be some slab of cement that had long ago been buried, but he doubted it. The sand on the surface was hard, like cement itself, and could not be scraped or swept aside. Camouflage.

"There better be a button or lever somewhere," Jasim muttered from the other side of the broad slab. "It's too deep or thick for me to simply dig down and pull on it."

"Yes," Leonidas said, continuing to follow its edge, also hoping a latch or control panel lay down here somewhere. The drone had gotten in somehow, but it might have had a radio transmitter.

As they worked, he glanced back often, hearing a groan or scrape as another pirate rose to his feet, looked around, then shambled off in the direction the others had fled. None of them had any fight left in them, but he wanted to make sure they wouldn't be trouble.

A couple of times during that skirmish, especially when the homemade cyborg had been battering him with those powerful blows, he'd had thoughts of home, of Alisa and the children. In the past, when engaged in a battle, he hadn't worried about anything except the fight, knowing that being distracted could get him killed, but in the past...he hadn't had a family somewhere else, a family that would wonder what happened to him if he slipped up and died. He knew Alisa would be fine financially, if he were to fall, but he loathed the idea of leaving her a widow once again. After all, she had lost her first husband during the war. He also loathed the idea of the twins growing up without a father. More than all that, he liked spending time with them, no matter how fraught they sometimes made him feel, and the idea of never being able to do that again, of dying here on this barren planet, was a distressing one. The excitement and anticipation he'd felt when he first left the *Nomad* to pursue this mission had disappeared, and he found himself longing for home rather than more battles.

Maybe this was why the empire hadn't wanted its cyborg soldiers to have families, people that they would worry about while on missions. People that would worry about them.

He hoped to finish this soon, so he could return home.

"I think I found something, sir." Jasim had moved up to a higher point on the slope, the top of the slab.

Leonidas forced his mind back to the present, to the threats they might still face. He would be more likely to return to his family in good health by keeping his focus on his mission.

Jasim appeared to push something a few times, then growled and pushed harder. A faint crack sounded, and Leonidas thought he'd broken whatever control panel he'd found, but a grinding noise came from under the sand, and the slab shuddered.

Leonidas jumped up and backed away. A clinking noise emanated from within the dune, and the top part of the slab pulled away from the slope and out over the sand, like the drawbridge of an Old Earth castle.

"That wasn't quiet," Jasim observed, looking back toward the *Interrogator*. "If he's in there, he likely knows we're here now."

"He probably knew we were here before the pirates even showed up." Leonidas looked toward the ship—Maddy had landed and said she would wait a little longer for them, but that they better not take all night. "Thinking of having your pilot fly up and blow up the dune?"

"It crossed my mind, but we don't know that he's in there, and there could be innocent workers. Nobody maintains a secret base by themselves, right?"

"He could have android or robot servants." Leonidas stepped onto the drawbridge and studied the wide, dark tunnel heading into the interior. Blowing up the dune might not do anything—the corridor sloped downward before disappearing around a dark bend. Whatever structure lay inside could be well under ground level.

"They're innocent too unless they have assholes for owners," Jasim said, hopping up next to him.

The drawbridge was sturdy enough for a vehicle to drive across—or a shuttle to land upon. Leonidas spotted a few dots on the sides of the corridor and pointed them out. "Those may be weapons—a security system."

"Good thing we've got our armor."

Leonidas did not point out that both of their suits had taken damage in the pirate skirmish, saying only, "Dufour may have anticipated that cyborgs in armor would eventually come visit him."

"You think he's installed measures that could trouble us," Jasim said, in a voice that suggested he did too.

"I'm sure he believes they can. And he may be right. Walking in the front door seems unwise. Comm your pilot, will you?"

"Maddy?" Jasim asked. "Your second-favorite cyborg has questions for you."

"Second?" Leonidas murmured.

"She doesn't know you that well yet."

"She's knitting me a hat."

"Because she's *already* knitted me a hat. Also a scarf." Jasim lowered his voice and mouthed, "They itch."

"What is it?" Maddy asked, her voice faint through Jasim's helmet.

"Ask her if the ship's sensors are able to detect anything now that the door is open. Also see if there are any differences in temperature around this dune. Now that it's night, and cooled off significantly, it might be possible to pick up something like an air conditioner or heater venting air."

Leonidas removed his helmet while Jasim spoke to her and took a few steps closer to the tunnel. He cocked an ear, listening to faint rumbles. A ventilation system, he guessed. If the house or base or whatever this was had been built completely underground, it would need fans to bring air in, which meant this wasn't likely the only opening.

He hopped off the drawbridge, put his helmet back on, and flicked to a heat-sensing view. His faceplate changed, showing blues, yellows, oranges, and reds against the contours of the dune. He walked along the top of it, peering down to either side, searching for disturbances that might indicate a vent.

"She says she doesn't see much, sir," Jasim said over the comm—he was still down by the drawbridge. "The sensors do show that there's something here now, with the door open, but there must be extensive shielding for the structure itself. The *Interrogator* can't penetrate it."

"Understood." Leonidas kept walking, making guesses about how long and wide a structure down there might be.

"Are you coming back down, sir? Should I close the door?"

Leonidas halted, spotting a temperature disturbance on the opposite side of the dune from the entrance. It was just below the ridge, and he scooted down to it, sand shifting underneath his boots. Warm air was escaping from what seemed to be the side of the dune. Any domicile down there should be cool, but Dufour might have refrigerators or other equipment that generated a lot of heat.

Leonidas brushed away sand, and his hand bumped against something—a camouflage mesh material covering a vent, protecting it from eyes and also from sand. His armor's sensors reported the temperature of the air blowing against his hand. It was several degrees warmer than the ambient air. He removed the vent covering and peered into a duct. Not surprisingly, it was too narrow for cyborg shoulders to fit through, but light was visible straight down, filtered through a screen, and he spotted a few more ducts running sideways from this main shaft.

"Sir?" Jasim asked.

"I'm over here." Leonidas crouched, considering the duct.

Between his blazer and his strength, he could widen the shaft, but it would make noise and take time. And there might be security measures in place down there, too. But would they be as strong as at the front entrance? And if Dufour heard noise, who would come to investigate? Him? Another human? Leonidas did not worry as much about human foes as technological ones, and it would be convenient if Dufour came to them. As long as Leonidas was in his armor, he shouldn't have to worry about a poison needle reaching his flesh. If the poison came as an aerosol, his suit would filter out any toxic elements before he inhaled them. He had already checked and was grateful his armor had only suffered dents and scorches during the battle—its integrity had not been breached.

Jasim's footsteps sounded in the sand behind him. "I wasn't sure if that was an invitation to join you, sir."

"What do you think of this hole?" Leonidas asked.

Jasim peered over his shoulder. "It's narrow."

"We could widen it." Leonidas gripped the side of the duct near the opening and applied enough force to press his fingers through the metal. It warped, then gave, and he pulled up a thin sheet, working slowly so he wouldn't make much noise. He thought cement or brick or some other hard material might line the shaft beneath it, but it was sandstone. A soft sandstone, he found, as he scraped into it with his gauntleted fingers. Particles broke away and sifted down the shaft. "Clay and gypsum, I'd guess. Like the sand out here."

"We're digging our way in then?" Jasim asked, sounding dubious.

"You object?" Leonidas pulled out another panel and tossed it to the side.

"Just aware that Maddy might not stick around all night waiting for us."

"Then we'll have to dig quickly." Leonidas dropped to his knees, breaking into the sandstone and trying to pull out the clumps he tore away, rather than letting them fall noisily onto the vent below.

Jasim grunted and knelt on the other side of the shaft to help. "Guess it can be practice for my next job."

"Teaching children?"

"No way to get a job like that, sir, like I said. I'll probably end up on someone's construction crew, carrying heavy things around. Digging holes."

"You have the same brain as any other human, Antar," Leonidas said, surprised that Jasim seemed so certain he couldn't do anything besides being a thug or a brute for a living. "Just because a few people have said no to your dreams doesn't mean they're unachievable."

"If you say so, sir."

Leonidas broke off and pulled up a large piece of sandstone. This would grow more difficult as they had to descend into the shaft to remove more as they went. Maybe they were being silly for not going in the front door.

The comm in Jasim's helmet beeped.

Leonidas paused, looking at him.

"Trouble," Maddy said tersely.

The squeal of blazer fire came from the other side of the dune.

Leonidas scrambled toward the ridge.

"The pirates came back?" Jasim whispered, coming behind him.

"Not exactly."

More weapons fire punctuated Maddy's words, followed by the roar of thrusters. The *Interrogator?*

Leonidas reached the ridge and crouched down, pulling Jasim down with him before he barreled over it.

"The ship needs help," he whispered, but he let Leonidas pull him down.

In the valley between the two dunes, the *Interrogator* was rising, the ship's thrusters flaring orange in the desert night. By their light, the attackers were visible. Numerous dark drones. These winged craft were far larger than the mail collection one had been. They flew around the ship like hungry raptors, firing as they darted in.

"It's fine for now," Leonidas said, pointing.

The shields were up, the blazer beams pinging off. Judging by the thickness of the energy blasts lighting up the night, those drones had blazers more powerful than hand weapons. Maddy wouldn't want to stick around, and Leonidas was about to tell Jasim to ask her to leave, but she must have figured that out. The *Interrogator* flew away from the dunes, heading in a direction that wouldn't take it—or its pursuers—over Leonidas's and Jasim's heads.

A few of the drones chased the ship while others swooped up and down the valley, skimming over the hovercraft wreckage. Looking for more enemies.

Leonidas pushed down on Jasim's shoulder as he sank low behind the ridge. He held a finger up to his faceplate in front of his mouth. Drones would be harder to fight than men. In addition to being able to keep out of reach, they might have shielding that would deflect blazer fire. Plus, there weren't many places for Leonidas and Jasim to take cover out here, unless they ran into the structure down there. Leonidas was sure they would only find more trouble inside.

Jasim must have realized he couldn't do anything to help his ship now, because he nodded and slumped down, a hand on his rifle as he watched the sky.

A humming came from the north as the drones that had taken off after the ship headed back. They were at a higher elevation than the ones searching the valley, so Leonidas flattened his back to the sand, his rifle ready. Their combat armor wouldn't give off heat and also had some sensor dampening capabilities, but if the drones had plain cameras and recorded their surroundings visually, they or someone watching the feed might notice the two dark lumps atop the lighter sand.

The hum increased as the drones came closer, one veering to fly along the ridge.

"I think I shook them," Maddy said over Jasim's helmet comm.

Leonidas heard it and winced at the noise. The helmet would have muffled the words to most people's ears, but who knew what the drones' capabilities were?

"But they hit *hard*," Maddy added. "I don't think it's safe for me to come back."

"Agreed," Jasim whispered. "We appreciate that you came back the last time."

She snorted. "As if you needed me. You two were taking down all those pirates all by yourselves. I barely got to shoot any."

"As a grandmother of twelve, should you sound so remorseful when you talk about not being able to kill people?"

"Thirteen, and pirates aren't people. They're vermin with the ability to talk. And not usually that well."

Leonidas made a cutting motion, and Jasim did not answer. The drone was almost overhead.

Leonidas did not rotate his helmet or twitch a finger. His shoulder blades itched as the armed construct sailed for their position. Had it seen them? Or sensed them?

Wind blew, scraping across the top of the ridge and battering their armor with sand. The drone cruised above them, and Leonidas mentally prepared himself for a fight. It seemed the thing could not possibly miss spotting them.

But drones did not have eyes, and their armor must not have registered on its scanners. It continued on, following the length of the ridge before swooping into the valley to join the others. One fired at a pirate, one that must have been too injured to get away. That seemed unfair, especially if Dufour had been the one to invite the pirates here to deal with his intruders. But maybe the drones were programmed to keep *everyone* away from the facility.

"I'll wait back at the cantina for you," Maddy said.

"When did you decide we're worth waiting for?" Jasim murmured.

"I haven't decided that, so be quick."

"We will, but don't forget, you promised Leonidas a hat. He would be chagrined if he didn't get it."

"I know he would. My hats are wonderful. I've informed my son-in-law that we're experiencing a few mechanical problems and will head to the next job as quickly as possible."

"Thank you, Maddy."

After a few minutes, the drones finished their search and sailed over the drawbridge and into the compound. A grinding reverberated through the dune, followed by a thump.

"I think the drawbridge just got raised," Jasim murmured.

Leonidas lifted his head. "Agreed. Back to digging."

"Don't you think…I mean, do you really think we can create a back door into the facility without alerting security? Some of those armed drones could be waiting at the bottom of the duct right now."

"Do you have a better plan?" Leonidas asked.

"No, sir."

CHAPTER THIRTEEN

"I can go first," Jasim whispered.

He was perched in the shaft above Leonidas, his feet and his hands planted on the rough sides they had carved out of the sandstone. It had taken most of an hour, but they had dug down to the vent at the bottom, pushing the stone out the top as they went. Jasim had been certain drones would descend upon them at any time, but the complex had fallen silent after the *Interrogator* flew away. Perhaps Dufour or whoever waited inside believed they had been driven off. Either that, or he was in there setting a trap. Jasim deemed that highly likely.

"That would be challenging considering you're behind me," Leonidas murmured as he reached for the vent, his fingers curling around the slats. Their suits' sensors did not read any life in the room that lay beneath the shaft, but that didn't mean much. The drones weren't living, and they were deadly.

"We could both climb out, and then I could go down first. Or you could push yourself to one side and let me squeeze past."

"That would involve a great deal of coziness," Leonidas said, "if not an impossible feat of gymnastics. My wife objects to me getting cozy with other people."

"Er." It still surprised Jasim when his former commander showed a sense of humor. "We're already ensconced in a dark nook together. An outside observer would assume a make-out session was already in progress."

"I'll go in first. You pause and make sure nothing kills me instantly. Get out of here if it does. If it doesn't seem that dangerous, jump down and back me up if there's a need to fight."

"Yes, sir," Jasim said, though his point in making the offer had been to avoid getting Leonidas killed instantly, or otherwise. Since he had a family to go back to, Jasim would prefer to ensure he was able to do so.

A soft clank came as Leonidas pulled the vent free. Bright light shone in the room below, and from up above him, Jasim could make out a cement floor littered with sand from their excavations and a drain, as if this were a locker room. He did not see any drones—yet.

There was nowhere to set the vent in the shaft, so Leonidas squeezed it, the metal groaning faintly as he bent it, first in half and then into quarters. He hopped down with it and his rifle in hand, landing in a crouch and doing a quick three-sixty.

Jasim scooted lower, prepared to jump down and help—no matter what happened, he wasn't leaving. But no sounds of a firefight broke out. Leonidas lowered his rifle and waved for Jasim to drop down.

A large room full of cabinets, workstations, and laboratory equipment opened up around them. A single door stood closed at one end. Several half-started projects lined the countertops, a mix of mechanical gadgets and liquids in high-tech chemistry apparatuses that Jasim couldn't name. Bags of powders and dark bottles of liquids rested here and there, labels warning of toxic and extremely dangerous contents. The sight sent a chill through Jasim. Was this where the killer manufactured his poisons? Poisons specifically designed to kill cyborgs?

As Leonidas walked toward a row of refrigeration units in the back, Jasim's comm made a feeble beep.

"Maddy?" he asked, glancing toward the row of statistics scrolling down his faceplate to affirm that someone had indeed opened communications.

A garbled stream of nonsense sounded in his ear.

"Uh, can you repeat that, please?" Remembering that some kind of sensor shielding had kept the ship from detecting the facility, Jasim moved directly under the open shaft. Would he have to climb out to speak with her?

"…message…your friend." That was Maddy, but her voice remained garbled. "The skip…"

"McCall sent more information?"

"Trans…receive?"

"I haven't received anything." Jasim started to tell Leonidas that he needed to climb out, but his display flashed, alerting him to a file received. "Never mind. I got it."

"…working…tassels. Out."

The comm fell silent.

"An update?" Leonidas asked, now walking along one of the counters, examining but not touching the equipment and projects lined up along it.

"On your hat? I believe so, but more importantly, McCall sent some more information." Jasim murmured a command to open the file.

"I am expecting a very grandiose hat."

"Good, because Maddy doesn't do understated or subtle." Jasim skimmed the words that came up, enlarging them to fill more of his face-plate. "It's a text file. About Dufour. McCall found birth information and, hm. That would explain why he hates cyborgs."

"Share it," Leonidas said.

"Terrance Dufour, son of Mary and Gabin Dufour, born in—damn, he's only nineteen years old? Can that be right?" Jasim looked around the laboratory at all the supplies and equipment, little of which he could have identified without labels.

"He may not be the only person involved."

"Right. Anyway, it says his father was a technician who worked for the empire for many years but then joined the Alliance and became an officer in their fleet when the war started. His wife had died years earlier in the chaos at—ah, she was at the Perun Arcade Massacre, a teacher trying to get the students to leave before things escalated."

Leonidas sighed. "That event created a lot of Alliance loyalists."

"Yes, so Terrance would have just been a kid for that, and then…he was fourteen when his father was killed. At Red Dawn Station." The more Jasim read, the more he suspected this Terrance Dufour *was* the only person involved, or at least was the person spearheading things.

"The battle for it? I was there. A lot of us were."

"The files doesn't say how exactly the father died," Jasim said, "but if one of us, or a squadron of our people, was responsible, that could explain why Dufour has a vendetta against us now."

"Yes."

"It probably has nothing to do with getting rich selling our implants. I bet he's only doing that to fund everything else. Sir…" Jasim closed his eyes. He didn't want to whine, but all of his desire for avenging his fallen brethren was bleeding out of him. Yes, nineteen was considered an adult, both in what remained of the empire and also on the new Alliance planets, but he remembered how stupid *he'd* been at nineteen. Hells, that was when he'd signed up for the cyborg surgery, a choice he'd soon thereafter come to regret. "I don't want to kill a teenage kid," he said quietly.

Leonidas did not respond. Maybe he was too busy thinking about how he'd come along on this mission with a pansy. Dufour had proven himself an enemy by murdering cyborgs long after the war ended and treaties had been signed. Jasim should simply accept that this had to be done, that the threat had to be ended.

Still, he found himself blurting, "Maybe we can just arrest him."

"To be thrown into what prison?" Leonidas asked quietly. He didn't sound cold and unsympathetic, but he also didn't sound like he would yield in this—he wouldn't leave someone out here who was hunting their kind.

"We could take him to a jail on Perun. The empire, even if Perun is all that's left of it, and it isn't really our empire, should be willing to incarcerate someone who's been killing former imperial soldiers. One was even killed *on* Perun."

"The Alliance has an extradition treaty with Perun. If his father was an officer, he would be entitled to an Alliance citizen's rights. They would take him back to stand trial on an Alliance planet. And—" Leonidas's voice grew softer, "—they would let him walk away. There might not even *be* a trial."

Jasim's shoulders slumped. "Right, and Dustor certainly wouldn't care—I think all they've got are debtors prisoners here anyway. You're shot for greater crimes. Damn, if we could lock him up, and he wasn't a threat anymore, that would be ideal."

"We can decide what to do with him after we find him." Something about the firmness in Leonidas's voice suggested he still thought that a blazer bolt to the forehead would be the best way to deal with the kid. "I have a feeling he's not here."

"Oh?" Jasim looked toward the still-closed door of the lab.

"I think he would have gone out to check on that pirate fight—and the drones chasing off your ship—if he had been here. This could just be his manufacturing facility." Leonidas looked grimly toward the counters.

"He had his mail brought here."

"Business address."

"What if we destroy the facility then?" Jasim asked. "That could keep him from manufacturing more poison, at least for a time."

"But only for a time. If he did this once, he could do it again. Also, I haven't seen the needles yet or anything that looks like the bronze drone."

"What should we do then?"

"Finish looking around. If he's not here, we may find clues to where he is. If we find some of the drones that have been delivering the poison, I'll be happy to destroy them. I'm not opposed to blowing up the rest of the facility, either, but let's see if any people are here first and gauge whether doing so would truly help keep the rest of the cyborgs alive."

"Yes, sir."

———

The underground facility was creepy. Jasim doubted fearless former soldiers were supposed to find things creepy, but he did, nonetheless. Once they left the lab, entering dark sandstone tunnels, there wasn't any light. Faint clinks and thunks sounded in the distance, and he didn't know if they were security constructs, poised to attack, or if the place had a noisy HVAC system. Air turned on with a hiss, blowing from vents in the walls. His suit monitors did not report anything inimical coming out, but Jasim could imagine their teenage mad scientist gassing intruders as part of his security system.

Leonidas led the way, despite the handful of offers Jasim had now made, offering to lead. Was it just because Leonidas considered himself someone who led—always—as well as giving commands? Or was it out of a lack of trust? Was there a question in Leonidas's mind that Jasim would do the right thing if he came face to face with the murderer first?

He thought he'd handled himself adequately with the pirates and the bikers on the station, but maybe Leonidas felt otherwise, or still remembered him as the kid who'd tried to weasel his way out of the military.

Maybe nothing Jasim did here or anywhere else would change his former commander's opinion. Or maybe there was nothing to change—maybe Leonidas's opinion was the correct one. Jasim's suggestion that they capture the cyborg murderer instead of killing him might have only reinforced it, that he wasn't suited to be a soldier—and never had been.

Leonidas paused at doorways, searching storage and equipment rooms, as if he sought some further clue or advantage to use on their enemy. Maybe he did.

"Sir?" Jasim asked.

"What?" Leonidas stepped out of an empty room. A lot of the rooms were empty or sparsely furnished. Maybe Dufour had bought the place used from some other mad scientist, one with more belongings.

"I never got a chance to say…back when I came to your office with Captain Goldkorn…I shouldn't have done that. Shouldn't have asked to get out."

Leonidas peered into another room and did not respond. Maybe he didn't care. He continued to the next room.

"That stuff about being depressed…it was true, I guess, but it wasn't anything worse than a lot of the men were dealing with. I just hated the killing. I didn't have the stomach for it. I didn't like much about military life, as I learned too late to change my mind, but the killing was the worst. Looking at the sightless eyes of someone who'd just been alive, someone you had shot, someone with a family back home. It had me hating life, hating myself. I questioned why I had the right to my life when I was taking it from others, and…Well, there were a lot of reasons I wanted out. But looking back, I should have dealt with it. Endured until things were over, one way or another. I'm glad I survived the war, though when I'm not being selfish, I admit I'm not sure it's fair that I did when others who did more, others who were heroes and had a real love for life, didn't make it out."

"Is this the appropriate time for discussing this?" Leonidas asked.

"Probably not, sir. I tried to bring it up back on the ship, when we were sparring, but…it's easier to talk to your back than your face."

The darkness and their armor helped. It meant that even if Leonidas looked back at him, Jasim wouldn't see what was in his eyes.

They walked up a set of stairs. The clinks were growing louder. Jasim still couldn't tell what they signified, but they were definitely getting closer to them.

"Not everybody is cut out to be a soldier, Antar," Leonidas said. "Sometimes, that's not something you figure out until after you get in."

"I wish I'd figured it out before signing on for the cyborg surgery—and the twenty-year commitment. Before that, I'd never even seen battle though. I worked in the supply room in my first unit, ordered parts. Soldiering wasn't so bad then, even if it wasn't my dream job. It was peaceful after the streets."

Leonidas did not respond. Jasim wasn't sure what he'd expected him to say, or hoped he would say. That Jasim wasn't a coward? That he hadn't been an embarrassment to the Corps? That he was a good man?

He sighed. As Leonidas had said, this wasn't the time for this.

The next door, one to their right side at the top of the stairs, did not open when Leonidas stood in front of the sensor. He waved his hand, but nothing happened. He punched the panel with his fist, startling Jasim. The door issued a peeved hiss and did not open.

"I'll get it, sir." Jasim gripped the door with both hands and forced it open.

Lights came on, revealing a big bedroom with an office area and decorations all over the walls. Posters from some of the popular vid releases of the last few years. There was a drum set in a corner with a mural of a band stuck to the wall behind it. The bed didn't look like it had ever been made, and the faint odor of sweat suggested the owner should do laundry more often. Overall, it looked like a kid's room. Even the office part. Most of the surface of the desk was covered with models and toys.

Leonidas walked slowly to the desk and picked up a model being constructed from interlocking blocks. It appeared to be a spaceship or rocket.

"Zizblocks," Leonidas said, an odd note in his voice.

"Sir?"

Leonidas set the model back down. "Prince Thorian used to build things with them."

"Oh." Jasim had never even seen the prince in person. "I didn't realize you knew him, sir."

"For a short time. I haven't heard from him in a while." Was that regret in his voice?

Jasim couldn't guess at the meaning of it. He remembered Emperor Markus coming to talk to the unit once, but he hadn't stayed long, and his son—there had been two sons then—hadn't been there.

"It is unfortunate," Leonidas said, a distant look in his eyes as he gazed around the room, "that children often suffer the most in war."

Jasim had a feeling he was thinking of someone besides Dufour, but was relieved to hear the sentiment from him. "I agree, sir. And they grow up full of hatred, full of seeds of bitterness that will germinate one day."

Leonidas looked at him. "Germinating seeds, Antar? Is that symbolism? You *should* be a teacher."

Jasim felt his cheeks warm. It didn't sound like a compliment.

But Leonidas thumped him on the arm as he headed for the door, adding, "Or perhaps a poet."

"I don't think that pays real well, sir."

"Probably about the same as teaching," Leonidas said dryly.

Jasim started to turn after him, but something sticking out from under a paper on the desk caught his eye. He stepped over to see what it was. The paper held directions to assembling the model spaceship. He moved it, and his breath caught.

Eight needles lay in a row on the corner of the desk. They were identical to the one Jasim had found in Banding's pawnshop and to the one that had protruded from that drone on Primus 7.

"Sir," he whispered and crouched for a closer look, trying to tell if poison gleamed on the needles' tips.

They appeared bare. For now. Did their presence here mean that the poison was stored in this room too? And what about the drones? Was there a storage cabinet full of them somewhere?

Leonidas returned to Jasim's side, looking grimly at the needles.

"We might want to search the room more thoroughly," Jasim said.

"Perhaps so."

Jasim looked under the bed while Leonidas poked through a closet. They searched bookcases full of comics and meatier tomes. The kid had a love for physical media. Jasim wondered if he had been alone since his father died, taking care of himself since age fourteen, much as Jasim had taken care of himself on the streets. Only this kid had done a better job if he'd made enough money to accumulate these belongings and this place—that couldn't have all been done since he'd started selling cyborg implants.

"Quit turning him into a person," Jasim muttered to himself. It would only make it that much harder to do what had to be done. The only logical thing they could do to keep their people safe.

He pulled a box out from under the bed and peered into it, finding old action figures.

A distant cry, almost a savage roar, sounded. Jasim dropped the box. Leonidas spun toward the door, though the cry had sounded like it came from somewhere deeper in the facility, on the lower level perhaps.

"I thought you said our target wasn't home," Jasim murmured, rising to his feet.

"I may have been wrong. Or he may have just arrived and found out about his intruders." Leonidas strode out of the room.

Jasim followed, though he wasn't sure what they'd heard had sounded like the cry of someone who had spotted cyborgs on the security cameras. But if it hadn't been Dufour, who else could it have been?

CHAPTER FOURTEEN

Rather than going back down the same stairs they had come up, Jasim and Leonidas found a second set of stairs heading down, and Leonidas did not hesitate to take them. He, too, must have thought the cry had come from somewhere on the lower level. Silence had fallen over the compound again, save for those distant clinking noises, and the cry had not repeated. If he had been alone, Jasim might have believed it had been his imagination.

They crept into a surprisingly wide and high corridor at the bottom of the stairs, one that looked like it had been designed for vehicles rather than people. It went left and right from the steps, but Leonidas picked the right option without hesitating. Only when they had traveled fifty or sixty feet did he hold up a hand. It was dark, and they were relying again on their night vision, so fine details weren't visible, but he pointed to a bump on the wall a few inches off the ground. There was a second similar one on the opposite side. He made a point of stepping over the invisible line between them. Jasim did the same.

There were three more spots like that and no doors until they reached a wide double door in the side wall. Grease spots stained the floor, and Jasim's armor sensors reported a faint draft stirring the air.

"Do you think that leads to the drawbridge?" he whispered, pointing past the door and up the passage. He'd gotten turned around and did not know where they were in relation to the entrance.

"Yes." Leonidas faced the closed double doors and a control panel next to them. He touched his hand to one of them, though he didn't force it open. He just stood there.

Curious, Jasim placed his palm on the door too. Like almost everything else in the compound, it was made of sandstone. Though his tactile senses were dulled by the gauntlet on his hand, he felt faint reverberations through the stone. The clinks he'd been hearing all along. They were louder down here.

"We forcing it open?" Jasim asked.

Leonidas tapped a few buttons on the control panel. A retina scanner beam appeared, encountered his faceplate, and flashed red.

"I believe so," Leonidas said. "You stand back and be ready to shoot." He waved Jasim to the wall opposite the doors.

Leonidas pressed his shoulder against one and heaved. Cyborgs could usually make short work of standard doors, but these heavy stone ones did not budge easily. Finally, something snapped, and a groan sounded as the door inched open.

Jasim came up behind him, pointing his rifle into the darkness within. Lights came on, illuminating a cavernous space, and he tensed. Since hearing that cry, that human cry, he'd worried about running into more than drones.

The large space, however, was empty. Some kind of vehicle garage, it must have taken up half of the square footage of the compound, if not more. A few closed rollup doors on the long wall opposite the entrance looked like they could hide hovercraft, autos, or even small ships. The clinking noise seemed to be coming from behind one of them. Some vehicle or machine that had been left running? Perhaps one of the reasons for the fans venting the air. Maybe the kid fixed thrust bikes in his spare time.

Leonidas eyed the big door where the clinking came from, but not for long. He turned toward the far wall. It was made of windows and showed a glimpse of some dark interior room.

A faint pained groan came from that direction, and the hairs on the back of Jasim's neck rose. There was a clear door between all those windows, a closed door. He doubted someone without enhanced hearing would have heard the groan, but Leonidas looked over, meeting his eyes. He jerked his chin in that direction, and they started forward.

"You don't think the kid stabbed himself with one of his own needles, do you?" Jasim whispered.

Leonidas shook his head once. Jasim remembered why he'd thought his old commander aloof—and had nearly wet himself the time he'd gone into his office.

The room at the far end remained dark as they continued toward it. Jasim looked back toward the door Leonidas had pushed open. The big garage did not have any other obvious exits, not unless he was wrong and those side doors led somewhere instead of housing vehicles. It crossed his mind that they could be easily trapped in here.

He reminded himself that he and Leonidas could tear down the walls if they needed to escape.

Another groan sounded, almost a whimper. Now Jasim could hear pained breathing through the door.

Leonidas reached it first, and Jasim silently admitted to being glad he was leading. This place—and those noises—made him uneasy. He had the feeling that they were being watched and eyed the walls, surprised he did not spot cameras along them. Maybe the cameras were well camouflaged.

The door was not locked. Leonidas pushed it open, leading with his rifle. The lights came on, and Jasim jerked, almost gasping.

A man lay on a massive stone table, his muscular body splayed across it, with inches-thick chains hanging from equally thick shackles around his wrists and ankles. They were bolted to the floor with bolts big enough to keep an android from escaping. Or, Jasim realized as he looked at the man's face, a cyborg.

He recognized him: Corporal Banding. The pawnshop owner. His old colleague.

A giant metal block lay atop his torso, pinning him down. It, too, was chained and bolted to the floor, those chains so tight that they could not be shifted. The weight would have crushed the ribs of a normal man. Maybe his spine too. Banding lay there, his breathing shallow, his eyes squinted shut with pain. He appeared conscious but did not look over at Leonidas and Jasim, did not seem to notice that they had entered.

"Banding," Leonidas whispered, stepping forward.

He lifted a hand, as if to reach for one of the chains to break it, but he paused. Jasim walked up beside him and saw why. An IV was inserted into Banding's arm. It was one of several wires and tubes attached to him.

Stands holding fluid bags rested next to the table, and the wires trailed to computers, holodisplays floating Banding's vital statistics in the air. All manner of equipment stretched along the back wall beyond the table, including a bronze, spherical drone with a needle-stabbing mechanism sticking out of one end. It was the same as, or maybe an upgrade to, the one they'd seen at the station. Several unlabeled bottles also rested on that table. Poisons?

"Blessings of the Suns Trinity, Banding," Leonidas said. "Have they been experimenting on you?"

Banding's eyes never opened, and he never gave any sign that he knew they were there, but another pitiful moan escaped his lips.

Jasim swallowed. He had seen his comrades die in battle, but this was ignoble and somehow worse.

"Break the chains," Leonidas said, kneeling beside the one binding Banding's right wrist.

"What about the IVs?" Jasim knelt beside one of the leg chains, though the size of the thing daunted him. And it wasn't simple steel. "What is this, ahridium? You could build an entire spaceship hull with this much."

"I'm not sure what happens if we pull the IVs. They could be injecting poison into him, or that might have already been done, and they're what's keeping him alive to experiment on." Leonidas glanced at the one closest to him, the wire dangling from Banding's elbow, and for the first time, Jasim saw uncertainty in his old commander's eyes. "No doctor around to call. We'll have to risk getting him out of here and trying to find some sawbones in the city."

Angry at this indignity, Jasim gripped the chain, intending to break it apart with his gauntleted hands. But it *was* the material of spaceship hulls, light and incredibly strong. It bent before it broke, and even with his armor enhancing his strength, it took a lot of twisting and growling to snap the links. Dufour had designed the chains with cyborgs in mind. Jasim was sure of it.

A crack rang out as Leonidas broke the chain near the shackle. Banding would have to wear the thick metal bracelets until they could find someone with a blowtorch. Or a key.

"You're still as strong as a mountain, sir," Jasim said. "Don't let anyone call you old."

"Flattery, Antar?" Leonidas moved around the head of the table, careful to avoid the wires, and reached for the chain coming from Banding's other wrist.

"Do you object?"

"Not as much as you'd think."

"Maybe I should have tried it years ago when I was trying to get you to sign me out of the unit."

Leonidas gave him an exasperated look. "What you didn't know then, and apparently don't know now, if you're still irked with me over that, is that I didn't have the power to do that. You sign their contract; the empire figures it owns you. Once they'd invested all that money and time in the surgeries, there was no way they were going to let you walk before your twenty years. I'm not sure they planned for us to walk even then." Leonidas knelt to wrestle with the chain. "Not many of us made it to the end of the enlistment and got to test that theory."

Jasim's chain finally gave way, and he dropped it to the floor with a clunk, moving to the final one holding Banding down. "I wasn't irked, sir. And I'm not now either. Not with you. Maybe with myself. Sometimes, when you're dancing on a sun's surface, anything looks like a better option. Even a black hole. You don't realize until you're in it that maybe you should have waited for another opportunity to escape."

"A lot of people regretted joining. You weren't the only one. But once you've given your word, you're honor bound."

Yes, the colonel had been a man of honor, and he'd expected it from those around him. Jasim remembered that. He wondered if that had been the reason Leonidas had gotten angry with him all those years ago. Less because the Corps was hard and the killing was disturbing and more because Jasim had wanted to break his word to the empire, to pretend he hadn't signed that contract.

"Yes, sir. And like I said, I'm not mad. That's not why I've been bringing it up. I just wanted...I don't know. It's not why I got in touch with you, but it's been on my mind these last few days, that maybe while we're doing this...you'd see that I've changed. You'd see that I'm not someone who would willingly break my word, not now. I can be trusted."

"Why does my opinion even matter?"

"I don't know. I guess, maybe if I can change your mind, I figure I'll have a chance at changing other people's minds too. About what they think cyborgs are. About what they think I am." Jasim heaved, pulling the link apart with another snap.

"You get *your* opinion of yourself straight, and then you've got a shot at the rest."

Jasim started to argue that he didn't have a poor opinion of himself, but he groped for the conviction needed to say the words. Leonidas spoke again first.

"Now get the chains holding this block on top of him."

"Yes, sir."

Banding was far more important than opinions right now. Jasim could dwell on their discussion later.

"We'll check out that clinking next," Leonidas said, tilting his chin toward the cavernous garage.

Jasim had almost forgotten about it. "Yes, sir. Do you think—"

Light flashed in the back of the room, and they both spun in that direction. Several monitors that had been dormant had come to life, indicators blinking on previously quiet computer consoles.

"Security?" Jasim asked, looking at the broken chains. Only two remained intact, the two on the block.

"Maybe," Leonidas said, eyeing a couple of the monitors. They showed medical statistics rather than security information.

Banding's heart beat rapidly even though he barely appeared conscious. Jasim had no idea what the other statistics indicated.

"Hurry and finish," Leonidas said, pointing to the remaining chains. "I want to get him unhooked and off this table."

"Yes, sir." Jasim didn't have a clue when it came to IVs, so he would let Leonidas handle that.

"Wish I knew what this stuff was," Leonidas muttered, bending over one as Jasim worked at snapping another chain. "Is it keeping him sedated or keeping him alive?"

The console beeped, and a computer announced, "Increasing dosage."

"What?" Leonidas jerked straight, lifting his hands. "I didn't touch anything yet."

A pained gasp came from Banding's lips, and his back tried to arch. The block kept his torso pinned down, so only his neck came off the table.

Leonidas cursed and yanked out the IVs stabbing the veins in each of his arms. A spasm went through Banding. His eyes flew open, but only for a second, and he didn't see them, didn't register anything except pain. He stiffened, gasped one more time, then slumped back on the table.

"Banding?" Leonidas rested a hand on his chest.

"He flatlined," Jasim said, horror filling him as he stared at the monitor, the one that had been measuring his heartbeat.

"Damn it, what?" Leonidas looked at it and checked his pulse. "Maybe I just pulled out a wire attached to the monitor...No."

He swore again and moved as if to do chest compressions, but the block covered too much of Banding's torso. He roared and crouched so he could shove at it from below. Jasim rushed to help, but Leonidas heaved it upward, snapping the last chain by himself. It crashed off the table and to the floor, so loudly that Jasim was sure the noise could be heard all the way back at the cantina.

Leonidas pressed a palm to Banding's chest and leaned in for compressions, but an ominous clanking sound came from the garage. One of the big vehicle doors started rolling up.

CHAPTER FIFTEEN

The clinks grew louder as the door fully rolled up. Leonidas looked from Banding to the noise, back to Banding, and finally back toward the noise. With a frustrated growl, he snatched up his rifle and lunged toward the door.

Jasim was already moving around the table and met him there. Whatever final poison had been administered to Banding, he doubted there would be any bringing him back. It was a sobering thought. Jasim hadn't known Banding well and hadn't spoken to him in years, but if he and Leonidas couldn't handle what came through that big door, they could be facing the same end.

Leonidas led the way into the cavernous garage as the shadows stirred in the huge alcove and something stomped into view. The bulky tank-sized contraption had four articulating legs, a squat body, and a giant head, all made from metal, maybe the same, nearly indestructible metal as the chains. Weapons that Jasim couldn't identify bristled from the front and back of the body, custom-made ones, he was sure. His first thought was that this was the owner's giant security robot, a construct meant to come out and protect the place if an alarm was triggered, but he glimpsed movement behind Glastica or some other clear material comprising the front of the blocky head.

"There's someone in there," Jasim blurted, not sure if Leonidas had seen. The head of the mechanical beast was just shy of the twenty-foot ceiling—Jasim was surprised the towering machine had fit in the alcove behind that rollup door.

Leonidas had stopped a few meters outside the room where Banding lay, and he was eyeing the contraption, maybe looking for weaknesses. It turned to face them, and Jasim was tempted to fire first, to see if he could do damage before the person driving it started firing. But the Glastica was clear enough that he could see the man in there from this angle, shoulders and head visible above a control console. He had a young face. Even though Jasim hadn't seen a picture of Dufour yet, he knew in his heart that this was their nineteen-year-old enemy. The person who had been a kid when he'd lost his father to cyborgs in the war. Even with Banding's death fresh in his mind, knowing Dufour's past made him hesitate, made him feel guilty since the empire—his *people*—had started the kid down this path.

A faint hiss came from vents high up on the walls. A greenish substance flowed out into the garage.

"Gas," Leonidas said.

Jasim's suit soon confirmed that, the sensors flashing an alert and also an analysis.

"A toxic gas," he replied quietly, not wanting their enemy to hear their conversation. "But it won't harm us through our suits." Not unless their armor, which had taken damage during the pirate battle, leaked.

Jasim's heart lurched into his throat as he looked at the stats scrolling down his faceplate. No, suit integrity was still good.

"Unless it's corrosive," Leonidas growled. "But it shouldn't be, or it would be a danger to him too. That contraption looks like it's made of material similar to our armor."

A click came from the construct, and several weapon ports on its legs popped open.

Jasim twitched with surprise. For some reason, he'd expected the kid to talk to them first, to tell them why he was killing them. He wasn't sure why. It wasn't as if the other cyborgs had received any warning or explanation.

"Look out," Leonidas barked, and ran, first dodging so he wouldn't be right in front of the thing, and then sprinting toward the wall. He probably wanted to run around behind it and jump on where he could do some damage—and avoid fire.

Jasim dodged in the other direction, firing at the Glastica viewing port as he did. If he could draw their attacker's attention, Leonidas could get in close and do some real damage. Or so he thought. Four weapons fired at once, two blazer-like beams of blue energy and two rockets.

Jasim threw himself to the ground as the beams lanced toward him. Both rockets went toward Leonidas. One slammed into a rollup door as he passed it. It exploded, flames and light bursting forth. Jasim was too busy rolling away from those beams to see what happened next over there, but Leonidas's voice sounded over his comm.

"He's not afraid of blowing up his own compound," he said.

Jasim sprang to his feet in time to leap aside as more beams arrowed in his direction. It didn't look like his first attack had done anything—if that was simple Glastica, it had to be reinforced with something.

Leonidas flattened himself to the ground as another rocket zipped straight at him. It crashed into the wall just behind him, blowing up with a thunderous boom that rattled the entire compound.

Jasim fired at the construct as he ran along the long wall toward the exit, having a vague notion that he might fire from behind the cover of the door-jamb if he reached it. The cavernous garage was too open, and the construct must have had targeting software—he didn't believe the kid would be able to fire so many weapons at once, not with accuracy. Only their cyborg speed had kept them from being hit. So far.

Smoke filled the air, gray mingling with the green gas. Jasim fired again, aiming at the joints of the legs and the seams in the head and body, hoping to find a weak spot. But he might as well have been firing at a spaceship.

"The face should be the most vulnerable target," Leonidas said, a pained note to his voice. Had he been hit? He'd finally managed to get behind the construct, but since it had weapons on both sides, he wouldn't be safe unless he climbed atop its back.

"I've hit it, and it hasn't done anything," Jasim said, skidding to a stop as one of those rocket launchers pointed in his direction.

It fired, and he sprang backward. It cut off his dash for the exit, slamming into the wall in front of the door. Jasim returned fire instead of running away from the explosion—he trusted his armor to keep him safe, and maybe the flames and smoke would make it harder for their enemy to see and target him. Pieces of rock thudded into his back, and a crash sounded as the doorway collapsed.

"Try a sustained blast," Leonidas said. "No, wait." He lowered his voice so it was barely audible over the comm. "Distract him. I'll try to get up to the head."

Distract him? Wouldn't that be fun.

One of the rear rockets fired, driving Leonidas away from the back of the construct. It also swiveled and moved farther away. It was doing too good of a job of keeping track of both of them.

Jasim stepped away from the wall and the doorway—what remained of it—and the construct fired again, this time with the energy beams. He sprang away, zigzagging to be unpredictable. Even so, one of the beams clipped his shoulder. He felt it even through his armor, and text scrolled down his faceplate, warning him that his suit's integrity was in danger. And that the gas was still out there.

"Terrance," Jasim called, not sure that the kid would respond or even pay attention. He certainly hadn't wanted to have a conversation before he started shooting. "We know you've been killing cyborgs, and we've come to stop you. The war is over. What you're doing is a crime."

"What *you* did was a crime," came the prompt snarl, the voice sounding young even though it was muffled, coming out through some speaker in the machine. "You're the killers, the murderers. You think we all didn't know? You think we didn't see? The crime was that you were allowed to live after the war. The Alliance should have killed you all."

Jasim waved away smoke, hoping his suit's sensors would warn him if more attacks came his way—he could barely see the construct through the haze. Somehow, he knew their enemy was glaring in his direction, though.

"The men in the Cyborg Corps were following orders," Jasim said, not sure what tactic might convince the kid to stop firing. Maybe nothing would. Maybe he was just buying time for Leonidas. The hatred in Dufour's voice made it clear that the wounds were still raw for him, that the last five years hadn't dulled his pain.

"You think that's an excuse?" he cried. "For years and years, you executed criminal orders. You never stood up to the empire, never thought to question if you were doing the right thing."

"The Alliance rebels were the anarchists, the ones who started everything. We were defending the empire and the loyal citizens—"

"Bullshit. You were defending tyranny and oppression. You were wrong, and you killed people just because they dared speak their minds."

Jasim took a deep breath. He wouldn't get anywhere with this line of arguing. It was always impossible to convince the rebels—the Alliance—that they had been wrong, especially since they had ultimately won. Somehow, that had validated everything for them, made them forget their own crimes, all the bombings, all the innocents who had been killed because they'd chosen guerrilla tactics instead of fighting fair. The cyborgs had always faced people openly. But this kid wouldn't care, just as the rest of the Alliance believed what it chose to believe.

"Either way," Jasim said, "the war is over. It's been over for five years. Killing cyborgs now won't bring your parents back."

"It will *avenge* their deaths." Dufour frowned at some display to his side. "I see you back there, cyborg," he growled. "You think I can't count to two and keep track of both of you?"

Jasim waved at more smoke. He sure as hell couldn't. If not for his suit sensors, he wouldn't know that Leonidas had worked his way between the wall and the back of the construct again.

Dufour fired at him again, and Jasim cursed, stepping forward as a rocket exploded. Had Leonidas had time to react to that?

Jasim growled and fired at the Glastica, remembering Leonidas's order about sustained fire. If nothing else, it should draw the kid's attention back to him.

Unfortunately, it drew too much of his attention. Or maybe he was trying to get away from what Leonidas was planning. Either way, the construct lurched into motion, striding across the floor faster than Jasim expected. He leaped to the side as one of those ponderous legs tried to come down on him. Between the girth and weight, he wouldn't be surprised if it could put a crack in his armor. And right now, with that gas still swirling from the vents, a crack would be deadly.

He thought the construct might continue past, especially if Dufour was just trying to escape Leonidas, but it whirled and stalked after Jasim. No, it *ran* after Jasim. Those legs pounded down, cracking cement under them. He dodged and fired as he fled its path, raking its belly with blazer fire. The bolts bounced off, much as they would with combat armor.

Jasim lowered his rifle on its harness, turned, and sprang at one of those legs. It kept moving with him on it, but he grabbed the joint and yanked, trying to tear off something important.

Another boom sounded, fire flaring off to his left. He hadn't even seen the rocket launch. Was he safe under here? Something snapped as he kept digging into the gap between the top and bottom of the leg. He tore away a protective panel. Then the body lurched and dropped down.

He yelped and flung himself away. The legs folded, and the body dropped all the way to the ground. As fast as his reflexes were, he didn't get fully away. Its bug-like carapace smashed down on his hip and one leg. His armor held, but groaned ominously. And he was pinned. He tried to twist onto his side, so he could find more leverage to free himself.

"Keep talking to him," Leonidas ordered, his voice coming over the comm. Jasim had no idea where he was.

"Get off my back, mech," came the kid's voice out of the speaker.

Ah, that's where he was. Jasim could have done more if he hadn't been pinned. He shoved at the massive weight—he was lucky he wasn't being crushed right through his armor. What was he supposed to talk about with their enemy while smashed beneath it?

"Listen, Terrance," he called up, though he couldn't see the kid from his position. "We're people, the same as you. We fought in the war, yes, but now that it's over, we're just civilians doing jobs. You'd kill us when we're contributing to society?"

"What do you contribute, repo man?"

Jasim winced from more than the weight on him.

"I know what you do, what you *all* do," Dufour said. "The galaxy won't miss you."

"It's honest work. It's not murder. Not like what you're doing."

"You murdered my family!"

Jasim grumbled and shoved at the weight. Arguing with the kid wasn't getting him anywhere. He reminded himself that Leonidas just wanted him distracted, and Dufour was obliging by talking back, but he wished he could find something to say that would end this instead of further escalating it. As steely and unwavering as their enemy was, it still seemed Jasim should be able to find some way out of this without utterly destroying him. Though he wasn't sure if Leonidas would let Dufour walk away after what he'd done to Banding, after what he'd done to the others.

The massive construct shifted to its legs again, and Jasim rolled away. His armor groaned, and something snapped in his hip joint. He grimaced, glancing up toward those vents, toward where the greenish gas still flowed out, mingling with the gray smoke.

"You're right," Jasim called, aware of the construct spinning around—chasing Leonidas? "You're right, Terrance. The war was horrible, and the killing was horrible."

To his surprise, the construct spun further until it pointed at him and until he could see the kid's face through the Glastica. His machine seemed to be out of rockets, but those energy weapons pointing at him made him crouch, ready to spring away. Dufour probably wanted to shut him up, but on the chance he was listening, Jasim pressed on.

"We were responsible for a lot of the killing," he said, meeting Dufour's eyes through the window and the smoke. "We were following orders, and we weren't the ones making the decisions about where to fight and who, but I know that doesn't make it any easier for you, for the families of those who were killed. I don't know if I played a role in your father's death, but I am sorry for it."

"It's your fault," Dufour whispered, his voice so soft that Jasim barely heard it, even with the speaker amplifying it. "You didn't have to become a soldier, a mutant cyborg. You made that choice, and you chose to serve tyrants." His voice grew louder and steelier. "Now, you die."

The construct lurched forward, and two energy weapons fired. Jasim threw himself into a roll, determined not to be crushed by the damn thing again. He fired as he came up, intending to aim at the head, but the construct was already stomping after him with impressive speed. He ended up sprinting away, blue beams biting into the cement at his heels, hurling broken shards into the air. He glanced back, shooting over his shoulder, and stumbled when he spotted Leonidas.

He was sprawled atop the head of the construct, his own head almost scraping along the ceiling. Jasim held his fire, not wanting to hit him, especially when he saw how battered and charred Leonidas's armor was now. He must have been caught in some of those explosions.

"You die," Dufour repeated, a whisper again. He was looking straight at Jasim.

Expecting more blazer fire, Jasim zigzagged his path again, careful not to let himself get caught in a corner. But the construct spat a cylindrical object straight out of a hole under the head. Jasim dove away, but it exploded in the air. Oily brown liquid spattered everywhere. He recognized it right away: a rust bang. The corrosive acid could eat through spaceship hulls—and combat armor.

Jasim turned his dive into a roll, trying to gain as much momentum as he could, knowing he needed to escape those spatters. He jumped to his feet, firing and running at the rubble-filled doorway. If he'd been hit, he couldn't stay in this garage, not with that gas choking the air.

At first, he thought he might have evaded the spatters, but a flashing red alert appeared among the stats running down his faceplate. A suit breach.

"Sir, my suit's been breached," Jasim blurted, then held his breath. That gas was so toxic that contact might be enough to kill him, but he wouldn't make it worse by inhaling.

He reached the rubble blocking the door and cleared it by grabbing boulders and throwing them at the construct. It stomped after him, firing. If Leonidas didn't do something soon, Jasim wouldn't have an opportunity to dig out, to get far enough away before he took a breath...

As Jasim glanced back, checking on Leonidas's progress as he hurled boulders from the broken doorway, he spotted his comrade still atop the construct's head, using his blazer to slowly cut into the metal up there. Dufour must have realized he was up there, because his contraption stopped chasing after Jasim. The head came up, smashing Leonidas into the ceiling. Jasim winced in sympathy. He had the doorway cleared enough to run out into the corridor, but he paused. To run away and leave Leonidas here, possibly to be killed…it would be even worse than trying to get out of the army all those years ago. He had brought Leonidas here, endangered him.

To avoid the head smashes, Leonidas had swung down so that his legs hung in front of the viewing window. He was gripping something to keep from falling fully, but his bottom half dangled helplessly.

The head came up again, smashing his arms into the ceiling. Leonidas growled, but hung on. He kicked at the Glastica, trying to break it with his boot.

Jasim's lungs were starting to cry for air, but he turned his back on the corridor. He ran in and aimed at the Glastica. If Leonidas's armored kicks couldn't break it, it had to be reinforced to insane proportions, but surely a sustained blast had to do *something*. Eventually.

The kid was focused on Leonidas, trying to grind his arms into the ceiling. He didn't seem to see Jasim standing in front of him, firing at his window.

The construct's head came up in a final smash, and Leonidas yelled and let go. As he fell to the ground, Jasim's sustained blast finally made it through, puncturing a small hole in the Glastica. He stopped firing immediately. Leonidas glanced up and must have seen the hole, because he pointed to the cleared doorway and ran. Still holding his breath, and praying that would be enough to keep him alive, Jasim also raced for it. Leonidas waited for him, making sure he got out first, then followed.

As Jasim turned into the corridor, he glanced back. Dufour was stomping after them in the construct, but he seemed to have stopped steering it. His gaze was to the side, riveted to that hole.

Jasim didn't have time to run back to that lab and climb up the shaft to get out into the clean desert air. He hoped the wide corridor led to the drawbridge, as they'd guessed. Starved for air, his face flaming hot, he raced for the end, his focus narrow and tight. He was barely aware that Leonidas wasn't keeping up with him. Maybe his armor hadn't been breached, so he didn't need to hurry.

Jasim rounded a bend, and the drawbridge came into view ahead of him. Out of nowhere, white beams lanced from all directions, crisscrossing the corridor. The traps Leonidas had been worried about waited for them.

Jasim, with blackness encroaching on his vision, ran straight through them. They were stronger than rifle fire, and more alerts flashed across his faceplate. Something bit into one of his back seams, and he finally lost his air in an involuntary gasp of pain. A boom sounded, and the floor pitched and heaved. He kept running anyway, almost crashing into the drawbridge. He thrust his shoulder against it and heaved, not bothering to fiddle with the control panel at the side.

Fortunately, it gave way, chains clacking as they loosened, lowering the drawbridge. He flung himself out before it was fully down, stumbled off the end of it, and dropped into the sand. He yanked his helmet off and breathed deeply, tired of the damn alerts. He flopped back onto the sand. If he was going to die, he would rather do it in peace.

Several minutes passed as he lay there, looking up at the stars. The inside of his throat itched, and his skin burned where the breaches in his suit were, but his lungs didn't seize up, and his heart didn't stop. He gradually allowed himself to believe he had escaped without taking in a lethal amount of the poison. The back of his shoulder hurt more than any of the rest of him, the spot where that beam had caught him in the end. His armor would need to spend a week in its repair case.

He laughed to himself. But he was *alive*.

Footsteps sounded, and then a shadow blotted out the stars, Leonidas's armored head and shoulders.

"You alive?" Leonidas asked.

"Yes, sir," Jasim said, his voice hoarse. He felt like he'd been screaming for hours and thought wistfully of an Asteroid Icy and how nice the dessert would taste and feel trickling down his throat. "Did you see...ah, did the gas get him?"

Leonidas nodded. "He knew he was in trouble and made it out of his walking tank, but not out of the garage. I didn't have to do anything. His own gas got him."

Jasim couldn't manage a triumphant fist pump or anything like it, both because he was tired and because it didn't feel like a victory. When he'd been talking to the kid, he had been trying to distract him and not much more, but he'd meant what he said at the end. He was sorry, sorry for the people he'd killed for an emperor he barely knew and sorry that politics and governments hadn't worked to keep the system out of war to start with. All those smart people sitting in their offices, and nobody had been able to figure out a way to peace that didn't involve the deaths of millions. Memories of Banding dying on that stone table came to mind, and he wondered if this was truly over, or if his people would be targets again.

At least for now, it was over.

"I destroyed the poison and the distribution drone," Leonidas said.

"Good. How was your walk out? Did you appreciate that I'd triggered all the traps for you?"

"I did. My armor was already beaten up."

"Mine too. I doubt my case will be able to repair everything," Jasim said. "If this had been a job and we were repossessing something for my employer, he would be covering my repair bill. I suppose I'm on my own here."

Leonidas looked back into the compound. "Maybe there's a lien on the walking tank somewhere."

Jasim grunted. "I doubt it. That looked homemade. By someone who expected cyborgs to come visit him someday."

"We could sell his comic books."

"Are you making jokes, sir?" Jasim felt too bleak to try.

"Probably not well. I don't have the knack for it that my wife does." Leonidas lowered his hand. "Are you ready to go back?"

Jasim thought that lying in the sand for a while—perhaps the rest of the night—sounded just fine, but even after all they'd been through, he didn't want to whine or appear weak to his old commander. He grabbed his helmet, accepted the hand, and let Leonidas pull him to his feet.

"You did well," Leonidas said, shifting his grip to Jasim's shoulder. "And if it matters, I trusted that you would."

Jasim met his eyes through his faceplate, ashamed that he'd almost fled when his suit had been breached, had almost left Leonidas to fend for himself. But he hadn't. He'd stayed, even though it might have cost him his life. No words or trusts had been broken. He nodded, to Leonidas and to himself. "Thank you, sir."

Leonidas lowered his hand and looked toward the sky.

"Should we walk back to the cantina, or should I call Maddy?" Jasim asked.

"It's your choice. I enjoy an invigorating walk."

Jasim bit back a groan. Hadn't Leonidas been invigorated enough? Hells, he'd run half the way out here as it was.

"If we walk, she'll probably have time to finish your hat," Jasim said. "With all of its tassels."

"Maybe you should comm her to get us now."

"I think that's best."

EPILOGUE

Jasim sat in the co-pilot's seat as Maddy flew him and Leonidas out of Dustor's atmosphere and into space. He eyed the mostly finished hat sitting in the knitting basket, but didn't ask about its progress. The tassels, looking like a very colorful octopus's tentacles, were alarming, and were those *balls* dangling at the ends? Jasim was fairly certain Leonidas hoped Maddy wouldn't have time to complete it before they dropped him off at Starfall Station, their rendezvous point with his freighter. Little did Leonidas know that Maddy continued to pilot because she enjoyed it, not because she needed the money—that meant she could afford to send packages across the entire system if she needed to.

Leonidas came into the hatchway behind them, resting his hands on the jamb as he gazed over Maddy's head and to the stars on the view screen. His armor was stashed away in its case, repairing itself the best it could. Like Jasim, he would need to visit a smith before his next battle. Unlike Jasim, he probably had the money to pay for it easily. Jasim hoped he would still have a job when he checked in later with The Pulverizer, though something about this whole adventure, or perhaps misadventure, had left him ready to go look for new work. Meaningful work. Work where his actions would help people, or at least never cause them to want to avenge themselves upon him and those he cared about.

"I received several messages while we were downside," Leonidas said.

"About what?"

"Many of our former colleagues got my warnings and offered to drop everything to come help us."

Our colleagues. Jasim felt heartened that Leonidas considered him a colleague, not some former subordinate with the appeal of gum stuck to the bottom of his boot.

"I believe the expression is better late than never," he said.

"Pah, late is too late," Maddy said. "Good thing you had me."

"It was indeed." Leonidas smiled faintly at Jasim and rested a hand on her shoulder.

Maddy beamed back at him. Jasim shook his head ruefully, fairly certain Leonidas had just assured that hat would find its way to him, no matter how far out in the system his freighter flew. Perhaps a scarf too. The consequences of being pleasant. A word Jasim never thought he would attribute to his old commander.

"What are you repossessing next?" Leonidas asked him.

"There's still a yacht waiting for us," Maddy said. "A real beauty from what I saw in the vids. I might have to try one of the bathtubs and rub myself all over one of those big beds with its luxury sheets before we take it back to Earl."

Leonidas blinked at the back of her head and lowered his hand.

"Pilots are an odd lot," Jasim told him.

"I've noticed that before."

Maddy flicked a hand toward them. "Nobody's odder than you cyborgs."

"If you get tired of repossessing yachts," Leonidas told Jasim, "I might know someone somewhere who could help you land a position in your chosen field."

Jasim swallowed, touched by the offer, if only because it meant that, somewhere along the way, Leonidas had decided he was worth helping.

"Or," Leonidas continued, "you could go into business for yourself."

"As a teacher?" Jasim hadn't heard of many entrepreneurial teachers and couldn't imagine how it would work.

"Our science officer—the lady you met at the station—records informative videos about her interests and puts them on the sys-net. She has all manner of people who watch them and request private tutoring sessions with her."

"Your freighter has a science officer?" Maddy asked while Jasim mulled over Leonidas's suggestion.

"Technically, she's also our children's tutor, but she's had numerous opportunities to pursue her research while aboard the ship. Our travels sometimes take us to interesting parts of the system. She enjoys studying the local flora and fauna. And fungi."

"Is that what she teaches about?" Jasim asked.

Leonidas hesitated. "More or less."

Jasim arched his brows, suspecting he wasn't getting the full story. What *were* worm castings for, anyway?

"I'll send you her sys-net island, and you can visit it, watch her vids. Get some ideas, maybe. Though I suggest you teach something *you're* passionate about."

"I got my best marks in early childhood education and psychology. And physical education." Jasim waved at one of his meaty arms, his lips twisting wryly. How not?

"Teaching exercises or self-defense would perhaps be an obvious choice, and it would certainly be easy to establish yourself as an authority on the subject. But—" Leonidas's eyes glinted with amusement, "—a hulking cyborg giving children tips on reading and math could be enough of a novelty that people would talk about it, spread the word."

"Hm." Jasim had to admit the idea had some appeal. He had never imagined himself teaching over the sys-net instead of in person, but he could start recording videos while still working in his current employment, and thus have the security of an income while making a name for himself in the education field. Also, children—and parents—might be far less intimidated by him if they were interacting with him through a video pickup instead of in person. Maybe he could even wear one of Maddy's tasseled hats to appear less threatening.

"The next time you have leave from work," Leonidas said, "and after you've figured out a curriculum for an initial series of videos, you could come out to the *Nomad*. I have some students that you could teach, students who aren't even faintly intimidated by large men with big muscles. Or anything else."

Jasim almost gaped at him. He remembered Leonidas saying his wife had wanted to invite him to dinner, but nothing in the way he'd spoken had suggested he agreed with the notion. But now, an invitation to come out to his ship? Leonidas must truly have decided that Jasim was a worthwhile comrade, a worthwhile *person*. Maybe, just maybe, if Jasim could convince one stodgy military officer that he was worth working with, he could convince others. After feeling disillusioned and defeated for so long, he now found himself ready for the challenge.

"Thank you, sir," he said. "Should I bring splat pads and whoopee cushions?"

Leonidas's eyes narrowed.

"To amuse the children and win them over to my side," Jasim explained.

"Well, that would probably win my *wife* over to your side."

"It sounds like you're surrounded by comedians," Jasim said. "Perhaps that's what has allowed you to develop a sense of humor. You weren't known for that back in the battalion, you know."

Leonidas lifted his chin. "Those among the upper echelon were not unaware of my wit."

"No doubt why we so often heard raucous laughter coming from the officers' billets," Jasim said dryly, distinctively *not* remembering that.

"Ah, there we go," Maddy said, turning in her seat and reaching for the knitting basket. "The autopilot is engaged. Now I can get back to my gift. Cyborg, lower your big head down here, will you? I need to check my measurements."

"I can already tell the tassels need to be longer," Jasim said with a smirk.

Leonidas's already narrowed eyes narrowed further. Jasim seriously doubted any of the Cyborg Corps officers would attest to the former colonel having been witty back then. Despite the slitted eyes and the glare, Leonidas bent at the waist, lowering his head for Maddy. She whistled cheerfully as she placed the hat on his head.

"If you guest host any of my videos," Jasim said, "I expect you to wear that."

"I expect *you'll* be wearing one too," Leonidas said.

"I could knit a special one that would be sure to make children find you appealing," Maddy said, smiling at Jasim as she adjusted Leonidas's hat.

"Uh," Jasim said.

"An *excellent* idea," Leonidas said, the gleam returning to his eyes.

———

The tassels were obnoxious, but it was the puffy balls dangling at the ends of several of them that took the hat into the ridiculous category. Still, Leonidas donned it as he walked through the airlock tube toward the *Star Nomad*. The children would like it, assuming they were aboard. The freighter had already been docked at Starfall Station when the *Interrogator* had arrived. Alisa could have taken the family for a shopping trip or to see the sights, such as they were. Leonidas vaguely remembered a null gravity zoo featuring creatures adapted for the environment.

The sounds of laughter and shouts drifted to him, and he smiled. The children were home. Good. He had missed his family, far more than he expected, especially considering it had only been a couple of weeks. He almost laughed at himself, remembering how eager he had been to escape and have a side adventure. In the future, when he felt fraught, he would simply plan a short vacation that didn't involve killing people. And he would make sure to bring Alisa along. Jasim had been a capable comrade, but Alisa was capable, too, and she was someone he could confide his feelings in, his distress at losing old colleagues, his surprise at how well he remembered them all, even after years with little to no contact.

"Daddy's home," came an exuberant cry as soon as he stepped through the airlock hatch.

Maya and Nika were both there, drawing on the deck with paint sticks of various colors. And drawing on their faces and clothes, too, if those green and blue streaks were an indication. Leonidas hoped that was a parentally approved activity and that the paints washed off easily.

"With a hat," Nika cried.

The girls dropped their sticks and raced toward him. Leonidas swooped them up, one in each arm, where they could and did plant kisses on his cheeks. One moist palm patted his nose, and he suspected he would find a blue smudge there next time he passed a mirror. He murmured greetings to the girls, agreeing to a request that he join them for painting later, then lifted his head and nodded toward Ostberg, who was feeding the chickens and probably babysitting. He waved exuberantly. His face was smudged, too, though that looked more like chocolate than paint. The smell of cookies baking wafted down from the mess hall. Jelena skipped out onto the walkway, carrying a plate, and his nostrils twitched in that direction. He had shared his brownies with Maddy and Jasim, so they had disappeared a while ago. Hard-working cyborgs needed a steady supply of baked goods.

"What have you two been doing?" Leonidas asked the twins, who were already tugging on his tassels. Maya nibbled experimentally on one of the goofy balls. She hadn't grown out of her phase of putting everything into her mouth yet. He hoped there weren't any chemicals in the wool.

"Art," Nika said proudly, looking down at their scribbles from her new lofty perch.

"I appreciated the art you sent along with me," Leonidas said. He'd had no idea what the pictures denoted, but he'd appreciated them nonetheless.

Jelena set the cookie plate down on the stairs and came over and hugged him. He did his best to return the gesture while holding the twins. Jelena had written him a letter, much as her mother had, though the content had been significantly different from what Alisa had penned. Mostly highlighting the merits of bringing back a horse if he saw one. She'd had that passion for as long as he had known her, and he and Alisa were starting to wonder if she would choose to become a veterinarian or something else that involved working with animals as a career.

"No horses?" Jelena asked.

"Sorry, not on Dustor. I think they'd eat horses if they showed up there."

"Ew, Dad." Jelena swatted him.

"I did bring something," Leonidas said.

"Presents!" Nika said.

Maya was still sampling the tassel balls and did not comment. Maybe she thought they were like scoops of ice cream and would have different flavors.

"I told you," Jelena informed them, grinning and stepping back.

As he set the twins down and dipped into his jacket pockets, he was aware of Alisa strolling out onto the walkway. He handed bags of moon rock candies to Maya and Nika—safe items to go into their mouths—and they raced off to compare colors and flavors. Jelena raised her eyebrows.

"Are you too old to be interested in candy?" Leonidas asked.

"I don't know. What's the alternative?" Her gaze drifted upward to his hat. "Not that, I hope."

"This is a designer original. One of a kind."

"It's big."

"It was made to fit my head."

"That explains its size. I'm not sure it explains the tassels."

"I don't think anything explains the tassels." Leonidas opened his jacket, plucking a long tube from an inner pocket. "There was an artist on the station with some prints. She signed this one for you."

"Is it a horse?" Jelena grabbed the tube and popped open the end cap.

"Close. It's a space unicorn, which is apparently a flying horse with wings and a horn."

Jelena unrolled the print and examined it. "She's beautiful." She carefully returned it to the tube, then flung her arms around Leonidas. "I'm going to put her above my bunk. Thank you!"

She ran off, hopping over the plate of cookies, and bumping Alisa as they passed on the stairs.

Alisa picked up the plate and headed over.

"Are there going to be stories?" Nika called over, her words somewhat mangled as she chewed on the taffy insides of one of the moon rocks.

"Yes, at dinner," Leonidas said. That would give him time to edit out the gruesome details. Maybe he would simply tell the adventure of the pirate attack.

"Did you bring *me* anything?" Alisa asked, sashaying as she drew close, the plate prominently displayed.

Leonidas wasn't sure whether she meant to entice him with the cookies or with herself. Perhaps both. He was amenable to both, but he first plucked a cookie off the plate.

"I thought your gift could be the fact that I didn't bring a *real* horse," he said.

"Please, that's *your* gift. You'd have to shovel the droppings if we had a horse onboard."

"I? Is that a job for a security officer and co-owner of the business?"

"It's a job for the man with the biggest muscles."

Alisa set the cookie plate on a crate, stepped close, and laid a hand on his chest. To fondle his muscles, he thought with anticipation, but when her fingers drifted, it was to search inside his jacket pockets.

"Ah ha," she said, her hand grazing a pocket. "What's this? Something hard."

"Yes, and since the children are nearby, I'll refrain from making an innuendo about hardness."

Alisa snorted. "If you kept your innuendo equipment in your jacket pocket, I'd be truly alarmed at the alterations the imperials did to you when they were operating."

"But you'd still love me, right?"

"In an alarmed way." She slid her hand into the pocket and extracted three chocolate bars in fancy wrappings, then made appreciative noises as she checked the labels. Her tastes in sweets were more refined than the children's. Dark chocolate, high cocoa content, no jakloff or cow's milk, thank you. "Ah, orange, lemon, and asteroid crunch. Wonderful choices."

Her arms slid around his waist, and she kissed him. It was a tad more chaste than he would have preferred after more than two weeks apart, but they did have three-year-old witnesses. Later, they could get unchaste.

"Were you able to stop the murderer?" Alisa asked, leaning against him, her chest squishing nicely against his.

Memories of fighting Dufour came to mind, and of the horrified expression on his young face when he'd seen the leak and known the gas would kill him. Memories of watching Banding die on that table also came to him. He didn't regret any of the decisions he had made out there, but he did regret the way the war had turned out, the fact that his people were scapegoats and targets years later, just because they had implants and had been good at their jobs. Nobody, he presumed, was hunting down the hundreds of thousands of other imperial soldiers who had served the emperor.

"Yes," he murmured finally, aware of Alisa looking up at him. "We got him. And I was reminded how much the entire system hates cyborgs." He wondered if Jasim would take him up on his suggestion and start recording videos. In a small way, something as innocuous as that could start to change a few minds about cyborgs.

"Not the *entire* system," Alisa said, rubbing his back and smiling. "It's unfortunate there isn't a way for you to use chocolate to bribe the rest of the universe into loving you."

"Is *that* what won you over?" he asked his Alliance-loyal wife, a woman who would have been happy to shoot him when they first met. To be fair, he would have shot her without qualms too.

"Well, it certainly wasn't your charisma." Her gaze drifted toward the hat. "Or your taste in clothing."

"Careful. If you tease me about this fine garment, I'll insist on wearing it to bed with you."

"I'm not sure those tassels and balls would enhance your sexual allure."

"First, you insult my charisma and then my allure. I may not bring you chocolate again."

Her eyes widened in mock horror. "Oh dear. I better make reparations for my careless tongue." She turned, waving toward the stairs. "Why don't you accompany me to our cabin, where it's easier to do such things?"

"Gladly."

THE END

Made in the
USA
Middletown, DE